PATH OF DUTY

Robin Gordon Walker

Path of Duty

ROBIN GORDON WALKER

UMBRIA PRESS

Copyright © the Estate of Robin Gordon Walker

First published 2015 by
Umbria Press London SW15 5DP

www.umbriapress.co.uk

Printed and bound by
Ashford Colour Press, Gosport

ISBN Book. 978-1-910074-08-4
ISBN E-book . 978-1-910074-09-1

Publisher's Note

Robin Gordon Walker, my uncle, wrote this roman à clef in 1944, soon after he had left Wellington College, resigning as a Housemaster and head of the History sixth in sympathy with the dismissal of the College chaplain, a firm friend and someone who shared Robin's liberal views on how a traditional school like Wellington should be run. It is a very thinly disguised novel of his time at Wellington and the schism in Common Room which led to his departure. Robin tragically died in 1947, a few years later, leaving a young widow, Rosemary, and an unborn daughter, Margaret Susan.

....

I am most grateful for the assistance of my twin brother, his namesake Robin and an OW.

Anthony Fletcher, OW, has given great support in publication of this book. He has most kindly written a revealing Foreword setting the real events described in the novel *Path of Duty* in context. His more detailed and important Afterword sets out the salient details in the history of Wellington College, before, during and after Robin's experiences at the school.

....

"The Path of Duty is the way to Glory"

Motto on a set of gates at Wellington College, known as the Glory Gate, together with a plaque in memory of Robin Gordon Walker 1911-1947

....

ALAN GORDON WALKER, OW, Publisher, Umbria Press

Foreword

Robin Gordon Walker's roman ā clef novel is clearly his account of his last term summer 1943 at Wellington, with all names changed and set in a fictional barely disguised school. Robin was a pupil in the Hardinge from 1924-1928 before going to Balliol. He returned as a teacher in 1933 at the age of twenty-two and was seen as part of a reforming group of Common Room staff under FB Malim. Robin worked closely with Terence Worsley about modernisation of the school, together with the Chaplain, Geoffrey How.

The Wellington common room of these pre-war years was dominated by a number of the 'Old Guard' masters, some of whom had taught Robin a few years earlier when he was in the Hardinge. Five of the senior tutors liked to think that they ran the school and were fiercely protective of restrictive school traditions. This group included CM Hughes-Games, tutor to Giles Romilly and Wanstall, known as the 'Hun'. The modernising group welcomed the arrival of the youthful Bobby Longden, who became Master in 1937 He was a charismatic figure and welcomed change: he had not been a teacher before, but had come from Oxford and was an old Etonian - which worried some in Common room, including a subsequent Master, Gus Stainforth.

Robin's roman ā clef is the fullest account we have of the interactions between the Master, WH House, Robin, the Chaplain Geoffrey, the clique of about thirty boys close to Geoffrey, the history sixth headed by Robin and the Hardinge boys, where Robin was appointed tutor by Longden. Bobby Longden was tragically killed by a German bomb in 1940, causing disruption and dismay to the reformers, but relief to the 'Old Guard', when he was replaced by a more traditional Master, Harry Wilfred House. Some of the light which had shone under Longden was extinguished from the College.

Since 1938 when Longden appointed Geoffrey as chaplain, he and Robin had formed a close friendship based upon their liberalism, radicalism and attitude to the emotional life of the boys. Geoffrey had come from time working in London boys clubs: "boys of all ages he adored and made his interest and affection quite obvious". His clique of frequent visitors to his room was about thirty to forty.

Robin makes his position about boy love affairs quite clear, in which in several cases he was deeply involved, advising the boys concerned as the emotional dynamics of partnerships came to his notice. They need to work through their affairs, expressing their emotions in diverse ways as their personalities dictate. Robin and Geoffrey's roles are to support and advise, accepting their emotions at face value. He sees four levels of intimacy that various boys want and need: simply being in each other's company, going round arm in arm, going round holding hands, fantasies of or some realisation of kissing and embracing, in private if possible. Robin believes that to suppress or disapprove of these liaisons is counterproductive. Harry Spencer, a boy in the Hardinge, subsequently wrote in his memoir, *Lascombe*, "tutor [Robin] understood and was always looking for outlets for that adolescent fire to prove that understanding and encouragement could achieve more than a slavish sticking to the rules". Robin's advice to boys was not to worry about feelings for other boys, since in two years or so their affections would in most cases transfer naturally to girls.

There is nothing in this account which conflicts in any way with the view of Michael Howard, a distinguished Old Wellingtonian who was taught by Robin at College, that Robin "flirted outrageously with the more attractive boys" and that his "open affections were infinitely healthier than the pinched pederasty of some of the other masters" It also reveals the modern cultural world that Robin was introducing his boys to, by reading to them, lending books, having them spend much time in his room (recent OWs in the forces returned and stayed overnight sleeping on Cleopatra, his living room divan.)

All this was miles away from the 'Old Guard's' view of their young charges. Four of them became frequent visitors to the Master, HW House, in the years 1942-3 to complain along various lines about Geoffrey and to a lesser extent Robin. House had spoken with Geoffrey at the start of the year to explain his need to cooperate with 'Old Guard' tutors.

All boys were in some sense Geoffrey's parish and he believed his ministry included all their emotional issues as he became aware of them. He knew boys on late visits should have the tutor's permission and had evolved his own system of to whom he told what. Hardinge boys were entirely Robin's responsibility but sixth form historians were not, so there were clashes with tutors, in some cases about proportions of their time spent on games or work for an Oxbridge candidate. Parents could be inveigled into struggles for control of a boy away at College.

In the aftermath of Bobby Longden, House was struggling to hold the school together as he began to see that Geoffrey and Robin were in effect taking it over. He had no time to get to know particular boys; they did not come to him anyway. He knew his head boy was one of those who disliked the Chaplain, Geoffrey. House believed obvious disunity in the Common Room was very bad for school morale. He moved towards feeling he had no choice but to dismiss Geoffrey, writing to bishops, the so called Chapel affair. This, however, was peripheral to the main conflict, which was based on the reassertion by the 'Old Guard' (minus Wanstell from April 1943) of their 1930s "we run the school" attitude.

House made his decision and summoned Geoffrey to tell him that he was to leave, in the last week or so of the summer term. House was very tense but believed that Robin could be mollified. Geoffrey, stunned, accepted his departure and House's plan was that Geoffrey would attend summer camp as planned and say his goodbyes then. No announcement would be made to the school. What he did not reckon with was Robin's immediate departure in solidarity with Geoffrey.

Robin's autobiographical account in this novel of how he handled his own departure in the Hardinge is poignant. I believe Robin felt a real need to tell his story for posterity but this was the only way he felt able to do it. The time is right for this account to be brought into the open and published as part of a key period in the history of Wellington College.

ANTHONY FLETCHER,
June 2015

PART I

HOT SUMMER SATURDAY

CHAPTER ONE

Peter Campbell, war-time Housemaster and head of the History sixth form at Chelborough School was teaching, in his inimical style, the senior students in his class.

"It's no good at all. It's dreadful – it's terrible – 'Maria Theresa. the jewel crested. queen, with her quiver full of potentially righteous children.'"

"Hugh, my dear boy – really! And you practically promised me last time that you had given up this Woolworth's style for good. "John, you misery, stop reading the infamous Huxley and listen to Hugh's essay.

Campbell, paused and there was a moment's silence – not a very long moment.

"Well, anyway, I think it's rather good. It creates a picture for me." Michael flicked his forehead back as he spoke, but his hair fell back immediately when he dropped his head forward again.

"My dear Michael, really! Leaping to Hugh's defence. Get back into your books, Michael. Get back into your Higher Certificate. Master the seven causes for the growth of the cotton industry in the Southern States. It's all you're fit for."

Peter Campbell clipped the essay together and flung it, half corrected, to Hugh, who was sitting, silent, happy and a bit bemused in the front desk on the right. Hugh picked it up off the floor and decided he wouldn't try to decipher the hieroglyphic corrections. He just caught sight of "Marvellous opening but I suppose you'll ruin it all later on." This was scribbled against the first paragraph.

"Give it to me again on Monday, Hugh; I may feel stronger after struggling with parents all the weekend. By the way, am I going to be burdened by visits from any of yours? John, is your mother coming down with your jewel crested sister or anything awful? Shut your books, children. What would you like me to read?"

There was a lazy, hot, anticipatory stir. Books were lethargically shut, all except for Michael who slammed his. He always did. Peter Campbell was vocally exhausted and found no words. He was fiddling among the welter of books on his untidy desk.

"Somebody's stolen my Eliot," he shouted. "Is there no honesty, no esprit de corps, no team spirit? And he raised his legs and draped them over the desk. His brown corduroys were rather worn end shabby; still, it was the fourth year of the war. "Anyway, that will stop Michael asking for *Little Gidding*. "Well, what do you want?"

"Read us *The Waste Land.* You haven't read that to us since you read it three times running when we wore all in the Remove."

"My dear Harry, I tell you my Eliot's been stolen."

Harry crossed his knees and nibbled his pen. That's irritating. I feel just like *The Waste Land.* Still, there's nothing much to be done about it, especially as I've got his Eliot, but I damned well won't say anything about it now. If I go to get it, I shall miss whatever is going to be read. It's funny how much pleasanter poetry is when Campbell reads it, even though he never quite reads it as you would yourself. Harry, thwarted over *The Waste Land* offered no other suggestions. Anyway, it was terribly hot.

"Read us the two songs for Benjamin Britten in *Look Stranger.*"

"No – read *Time was away and somewhere else* – or something by MacNeice."

"Why not read some Robert Frost or that other American you read us last week – Strindberg or someone?"

"Oh well, perhaps this will do." Campbell lent back in his chair. It tipped up ominously on to its two back legs but somehow it never seemed to topple over. He stared out of the window over the cricket field. A match was going on but although you could hear the game you couldn't see it properly, because the sight screen blocked the view of the pitch. Occasionally the deep field moved out of sight and one vaguely realized that another over before lunch had been bowled. He looked back at the book. The ten budding scholars were leaning back, mostly with their legs up along the benches. They enjoyed last school on Saturday morning.

"Dickie, you'd rather be watching the cricket. You can go."

"No, I'd rather stay."

"All right then." Campbell began to read:

Young men walking the open streets
Of death's republic, remember your lovers...

"You aren't really listening, I'll begin again." Campbell nearly always began again. Harry could never make up his mind whether it was because somebody really wasn't listing or whether it was because he wasn't satisfied with the atmosphere he'd managed to create. Anyway, he began again and the room was dead quiet. This time Peter Campbell dwelt much longer on the word 'remember'.

Young men walking the open streets
Of death's republic, remember your lovers.
When you foresaw with vision prescient
The planet pain rising across your sky
We fused your sight in our soft burning beauty...

Harry was drinking in the words. It's funny how affected I am when it's a really fine poem. Peter Campbell's quiet whispering voice held his attention. Campbell was obviously nearing the end; his voice was very low. He always dropped his voice towards the end of a poem.

Young men who lie in the carven beds of death
Remember your lovers, who gave you more than dreams
From the sun sheltering your careless head
Or from the painted devil your quick eye,
He led you out of terror tenderly
And fooled you into peace with our soft words
And gave you all we had and let you die.
Young men, drunk with death's quenchable wisdom,
Remember your lovers who gave you more than love.

There was a pause, and Peter Campbell gazed a long way out of the window. What a fate to be a schoolmaster in war-time. Young men, in the carven beds or death, remember your lovers. Andrew will never forget Roger not at least till Andrew is killed himself. And Harry there, Harry is thinking of Bill, who left last term – I am sure of it. Nothing really is simpler than adolescent love, in spite of the efforts of most schoolmasters to begrime it, to leave that unnecessary dirty mark in the boy's mind.

"Well, children, do some work over the weekend. We don't seem to have got very much done today. You may go."

"Oh no. Just read one more. Read us *Cervieres*."

"No, children, no. And again I say no. I'm only a paid servant of the governors: 1½d a minute and no overtime. Why should I waste my efforts reading to you? I always stop punctually on time."

"Nonsense," muttered John. "It's five minutes past already. Still, if you won't I suppose you won't and that's that."

Slowly they collected their books. The scholarship history boys always moved lethargically. It was partly a pose, partly the result of their contact with the past, but mostly a pose.

Peter Campbell put on his gown inside out. You could always tell by the white tab announcing "Castell, Oxford." He didn't seem in the mood to linger, as he sometimes did, to talk to the others lingering. He walked out slowly and deliberately. He turned right, walked in isolation through the shabby courts down to watch the cricket till lunch. John, Harry and Michael, who were a well-known and slightly suspect trio, turned left and also wandered down, with their Huxleys, Joads and Maritains under their arms, through Carpenter's Gate, down the gravel road to the cricket field, and there lay on the grass to the right of the sight screen and they didn't seem to want to talk.,

CHAPTER TWO

Campbell went up to his rooms after lunch. He had been a Housemaster for three years and never found it very easy, although it was always delightful. The first quarter of an hour after lunch was spent fussing, signing leaves to go out with parents, signing leaves to go bicycling, all kinds of bits of paper needed signing, distributing money from the boys' "bank accounts" and so and so on. I can't very well write a letter to Mrs Wetherby to tell her that her boy is all right till I've been down to the Sanatorium to see him. I didn't go yesterday. I must go today. I'll go later on, and it doesn't matter if I don't catch the seven-o'clock post as it won't get there till Monday anyway. I wish Wetherby wasn't in a ward by himself; he is so tongue-tied.

A small boy came in.

"Well, miserable, why are you so late? And what do you want?"

"I want a stamp, sir."

"Well, I'm not a post office, you miserable little whippersnapper. I can't be open all day. How many times have I told you to come in directly after lunch?"

"Sorry, sir." The small boy didn't appear very alarmed.

"Sorrow's useless. Well, here's your stamp and I suppose you haven't got 2½d and want me to write it down against your account."

"Yes, sir, sorry, sir,"

Campbell fumbled with the keys and unlocked the drawer. The boy stood awkwardly with one finger dangling on the edge of the desk. Occasionally he lent on it as though in need of support. Campbell scribbled in the book.

"Are you very busy this afternoon, sir?

"Yes, of course. Why?"

"Only, George and Jerry and me thought we'd play tennis and we've got a court at four o'clock. Would you like to play sir?"

"Oh, Charlie, four o'clock is a terrible time. You know we old grown-ups like a cup of tea, and I've got Dickie's mother coming to see me at half past three. I don't see how I can possibly play at four, but I will play sometime. Try and get a court one Sunday. It's far easier for me on a Sunday. But are you any good? I can't believe Jerry's any good – because, you see, I really am rather good – but still I promise to play if you'll get a court on Sunday."

"Sir, have you any tennis balls?"

"Oh, so that's it. Yes, here you are, but don't lose them. You know how valuable they are nowadays. Five of them are marked P.C. for Peter Campbell, and. the other isn't marked at all so you'll have to keep an eye on it, but whilst keeping your clumsy great eyes on that one, don't lose the other five."

"Honestly, sir, it wasn't the balls we wanted, sir."

"No, I know, you miserable little rabbit. Don't take me any more seriously than you take yourself. By the way, ITMA's on tonight at seven. Are you and Charlie and company coming along?"

"Well sir, I don't know. I was thinking of going to the Junior Debate but I doubt if Charlie's going to it."

"Well. I shan't be here probably; so tell Charlie etc, to come along if they want to, or anyone else for that matter. I know you miseries like to know when my room's going to be unoccupied over the weekend, so that you can take possession. But no one's to come in tomorrow afternoon as some of those history boys are coming up to listen to some concert or other. Do buzz along now, and don't come in so late another time."

And the boy took his finger off the desk at last, swivelled round and went out.

I shall have to play with those brats one Sunday. It's silly really because you can't teach bad players much in a four, if you only play with them once in a while.

The door opened without a knock and John came in. He was the ablest member of Campbell's history sixth, but not in his House.

"I listened outside and there wasn't anyone inside."

John was very able intellectually but restless and unsettled. The war had disturbed him. He was a fine rugger player and cricketer and useful at hockey. He had vaguely curly hair, his lips pouted more often than not, and he had a cherry nose under misty eyes. Boys liked him in spite of his affected manner.

"Here's this essay, Campbell."

"Is it good?"

"I dunno; I thought it was when I wrote it but now it seems awful."

"Well, I'll have a look at it, but I don't think I shall be able to till tomorrow."

"Campbell, what are you doing this afternoon?"

"Does that mean you want me to do something with you, because if so, I'm terribly busy: in fact, I am busier than that."

"No, I just wondered if you were going to be in or out." John walked over to the bookcase and picked up a copper vase.

"You see I thought I'd like to read up here. It's so noisy in my House and it's difficult to read *Technics and Civilisation* in a noisy House."

"Quite – and then?"

"Well, and then I thought Michael and Harry might come up and we could all have tea."

"Does that include me?"

"Of course."

"Who provides the tea, John?"

"Well, I suppose you do mostly, but I've got a cake."

"Well, it's no good because I've got a parent coming at half past three."

"Oh, Campbell, you've got a parent coming! You're hopeless nowadays. What with your House and your parents, you might as well live on a desert island as far as we are concerned."

"Well, John, anyway you can read here till about three, because I'm going next door to lie on my bed and think, and then I'm going to watch the cricket with Mrs Dickie and talk to her, and then I'm going to watch my smalls practising for the gymnasium competition and then there are four Old Chelburians turning up and, as I've got no drink, I shall have to take them down to the 'Old Maid of Perth'. By the way, can you organise three bikes at the bottom of my stairs by quarter-past-six?"

"I should think so. Anyway, I'll try."

"Well. I'm off to lie down and think. I'll leave you, John, to read, and don't fool about with all these things on the floor. They are paper and cardboard models made by the Remove of the bedsitting-rooms they imagine that they'll have in their first year of grown-up freedom. Pretty expensive and ghastly tastes. Fourteen out of twenty have cocktail cabinets, and eleven have photos of school teams all around the walls. You see, I've got a lot of work to do with them. Still, they are a new lot and they'll improve and Gibbons and Raleigh write marvellously, and Shelley paints well and there's a good deal of musical talent about. They'll teach each other quite soon, if I give them air."

"Have you anything of theirs I could read?"

"Nothing terribly exciting. There's a wad over there on 'Pack up the Moon, Dismantle the Sun'. One or two are quite good, but I haven't read them all. Would you like to correct them for me, John? No, perhaps you'd better not. I don't know the miseries well enough yet and they'd probably be annoyed. Anyway, have a look at them and let me know what you think. Look here, I'm off to browse and meditate on my voluptuous bed. You, I suppose, will tuck yourself up on the divan surrounded with Cleopatra's cushions and read." Campbell's divan was always called "Cleopatra" or "Cleo".

"What are you going to meditate about, Campbell?"

"Oh, life and death I expect, and, if I told you more, that would be telling too much, wouldn't it?"

John collapsed on the divan and Campbell helped himself to one of his interminable cigarettes. He lit it off the stub of one he was still smoking, although it didn't appear as though the old one was nearly ready to be thrown away.

"Well, hey-ho, Campbell – meditate proudly and profoundly. I'll look at these 'Moons and Suns' first. Don't go to sleep before you've had any great thoughts."

"O.K. – hey ho – and I'll murder you if you put on the wireless."

Campbell went out and left the door ajar. He ambled down the passage, went into his bedroom, took off his coat, trousers and tie, stubbed out the newly lit cigarette, lay down on the bed and covered himself over with the green eiderdown.

CHAPTER THREE

The Chaplain's rooms were far away from Peter Campbell's House. This was always irksome as Richard Yates and Peter Campbell were often in consultation and had a lot of mutual friends both among the Old Chelburians and the boys. Standing in the courts after tea there was often an argument which room to go to. Campbell's room had the advantage of a radiogram and, before the war, lots of chocolate biscuits and lemon squash; but the disadvantage was that it tended to be full of boys from his own House and you really wanted to go to a master's room to meet all sorts of people from all sorts of Houses. Richard Yates' room, the Chaplain's room, had the advantage that there tended to be boys of all ages dropping in, and in more ways it was more fun.

That Saturday afternoon Harry and Michael – both of whom were in Campbell's history sixth – decided after lunch to go up to the Chaplain's room. "We'll go and beat up old Richard," they said.

They found the Chaplain, oddly enough, sitting at his desk, surrounded by little bits of paper and an enormous notebook. Some of the bits of paper blew off' the desk as they opened the door and landed on the derelict sofa.

"Shut that door, blast you," shrieked the Chaplain, "but thank goodness you've come. Where's John, have you drowned him or something?" Everybody always seemed to assume that Michael and Harry and John would be together.

"Oh, John said he was going up to see Campbell," said Harry, and Michael went on to finish the sentence. Michael had a tiresome way of finishing other people's sentences. "He said he's going to organise tea up there for us. Richard, you'll come too?"

"Yes, I'll come, of course I'll come. That will be lovely, and I'll bring Rowland and that new friend of his, I've forgotten his name. I'm glad Rowland's bringing him up – Rowland needs a friend very badly at the moment." There was no answer. "Well, he does, doesn't he? – or doesn't he?

Harry and Michael said nothing.

"Well, I'm sure he does," said the Chaplain. "I told his Housemaster, Watson, last night. He wasn't quite sure, but I think he does. He needs friendship – can't get on without it."

"Oh, I expect Watson wasn't sure, because the friend is in a different House," Harry said.

"Well, personally I think it should be encouraged, but I want to meet the other boy – because, though it may be good for Rowland, it mightn't be so good for the other boy. That's what always makes these things so difficult. You two can help. See what you think of him. Is he a boy who can look after himself, because, after all, sooner or later Rowland will suggest something pretty wild?"

Michael, by this time, was leaning over the Chaplain's shoulder.

"What on earth are you doing, Richard?'

"Masters' Room accounts. These are the drink and smoke bills for the end of last term. I've got to get them done by six o'clock. Sit down and help me add them up. No, no, perhaps you'd better not; I expect they are meant to be confidential. Almost everything to do with masters seems to be confidential."

"I can't see why they should be," Harry said. "If they are ashamed of drinking in the Masters' Room, then drinking shouldn't be allowed there. If they are not ashamed it can't be confidential."

"Well, unless we help you, you'll never get them done by six o'clock, especially if you've got Rowland and Co coming to tea. So we'd better get cracking" Michael seized a. block of paper and a wad of chits and started checking them off. Harry took some more and there were confused mumblings, foggy additions and muttered curses for about ten minutes. Then the strain was too much for Michael. Michael was Irish. He was a good-looking bumpkin type, with straight, unruly, protruding hair, blue eyes, a straight nose over a giggly mouth and a high windswept complexion which made him oddly attractive. He walked in an extraordinary way and seemed never to have complete control over both legs at once. As if to show that he wasn't interested in this failing, his trousers were always casually done up with an ineffective belt and this rather drew attention to the patches and tears he seemed to collect on his coat and trousers. Out of doors, unless the weather was unbearably hot, he always wore a bright blue and white woollen scarf thrown around his neck. It signified nothing, but it was fun and, for some extraordinary reason, although it was against the rules, no one had really tried to stop him.

Michael had once been working for an English scholarship but he had long since given that up. He had a lovely Irish lyric flair and wrote beautifully. He had retained, even at the age of seventeen and a half, the young boy's capacity for wonder, and he knew how to find words to express his experience and vision; but for Anglo Saxon and the exhaustions of historical spadework he had no use. His was spending his last term in trying to get a Higher Certificate. No one quite knew why, except that it was vaguely thought that it was good to tie him down to something. In point of fact, it was very difficult to see what good it would do him.

Michael was getting bored. "What an extraordinary amount of ginger-beer old "Rattlebones" drinks. Thirty-seven bottles in four weeks. I would burst if I drank that." 'Rattlebones" was the pet name for an aged master who was in no way a pet.

"No, you wouldn't," said Harry. "Anyway, it's probably better then Campbell: twenty-four gin and lemons and forty-seven beers."

"Yes," said the Chaplain, "but remember that includes Old Chelburian Day."

"Well, twenty-four gins in four weeks isn't enormous. My father drinks at least sixty, but of course, he has got a pink market source of supply!"

"What's happening about John and the cricket?" The Chaplain looked up at Michael as he spoke. His brick-red coloured shirt didn't seem at all incongruous in this room. The room was walled in with books. Many of them were religious books and the gaps in the religious bookcase showed that quite a. lot of them had been borrowed by the boys. One or two books in the next-door bookcase had lurid titles: *Twelve Chinks and a Woman*, *No Orchids for Miss Blandish*. The Chaplain firmly believed that all books which he has read, enjoyed and owned should be on view. He was not one of those who kept some books in his bedroom, out of sight. Not that it would have been much good in his case, as boys were just as likely to burst in on him in his bedroom as anywhere else.

Michael had picked up a *New Statesman*, but Harry was still adding audibly and desperately, so the Chaplain repeated his question.

"What's happening about John and the cricket?" I've thought a good deal about it. It would be a bit easier if John didn't insist on playing in House matches."

"Yes," piped in Michael who never kept out of a discussion for long. "But Tuesday's only one afternoon a week, and if he plays for the Eleven he has to give up three, and three whole afternoons plus all Saturday morning is a lot if you are really working. Anyway, why shouldn't he have some relaxation? And, though he is damned good, most people say he can be replaced in the Eleven, whereas Franklin's House team wouldn't exist without him. And no one can say it's cup-hunting because Franklin's have no hope at all, even with John."

"Yes, that's true but it does give people like M.C.C." – the cricket master was called M.C.C – "a chance to say that John's putting House before school, and in a kind of way he is. M.C.C. was saying so in the Masters' room yesterday.

"Well, Campbell told John – and Campbell's no fool and a cricketer – Campbell told John he was right. From the point of view of doing credit to the school a scholarship at King's is worth several centuries to any school that has a catholic sense of values – but John, or anyone else, need the relaxation of one carefree game a week, and playing cricket for the school certainly isn't carefree. Campbell said that he thought people were just venting their disappointment, their dislike of John's tendency to affectation and their slight suspicion of any scholarship pretensions." Harry kept on looking up and down as he was speaking.

"Yes, John's right and Campbell's right. Campbell isn't always right but he is this time – yes, of course he is." The Chaplain was desperately keen on John's scholarship and also keen, but not so keen, on his cricket. It was this that had delayed his normal impetuosity. Generally his decisions on right and wrong were instinctive and were uttered with machine-gun velocity.

"Well, do tell John, Richard. He's a little worried that you haven't said anything. He's sure you know all about this fuss and bother." Michael had a loyalty towards John that might have shamed David or Jonathan.

"Yes, I'll tell him at tea. I'll tell him."

The Chaplain seemed brighter – glad to have made up his mind. He wasn't used to indecision. Richard looked about twenty-eight and was actually thirty-nine. He had been in the Navy but was invalided out, the result of some bug he had picked up in South America. Then at the age of twenty-four he had gone into the Church. He dashed into an East London curacy with vigorous enthusiasm, which had never been damped or exhausted by close and intimate contact with numerous East End boys' clubs. He had accepted the appointment at Chelborough with some misgivings, partly because he felt the job was too easy-going and luxurious, partly because he knew that, during all his recent life, he had taken discipline very strictly at its face-value and he knew that it would be difficult not to reject some of the traditional discipline of a public school. Boys of all ages he adored and he made his interest and affection quite obvious. Some accused him of favouritism, because he saw a great deal of about thirty or forty boys in any one stretch of time. If taxed with it, he never denied it. His supporters pointed out that it was impossible for a man to deal helpfully with more than that number at any one moment, if he was going to get to know them well enough to assist them.

The greater number of boys at Chelborough loved and respected him. A few genuinely disliked him for what could be interpreted as favouritism; a few were jealous because they didn't know him better, but most of them liked his eyes, his clean-shaven face, his impetuous and self-revealing honesty and the interest he took in all school activities. He was to be seen everywhere – skating in winter, in summer in the swimming pool, whenever there was bathing, playing hockey, tennis, or cricket. All these he did badly because of his illness. It had affected his back. Yet he never seemed to resent the fact that he was no longer good, and his cheerful incompetence and sense of frolic made the boys love sharing their games with him – and boys don't always like to share their games with adults. Richard was equally contented when the boys were in the Art School, the Music Palace, or talking to them about horses or pictures or books.

Probably it was the fact that Richard always put the chapel first, possibly it was the fact that, to him, the Chapel was a friendly place for friends and friendship, or perhaps it was his unashamed sincerity that gained him his numerous following. Unlike so many, he never excused religion. He preached and taught such a discipline of the Church that his critics felt he might well have paid more respect to the discipline of the school. And the extraordinary thing was that, though he was fully aware of the influence he wielded among the boys, he never seemed really aware of his popularity. He wanted and needed the general affection of the boys, but never seemed to realize that he'd got it.

"Well, these accounts are pretty well done now, aren't they? I should think you could finish them in five minutes now, Richard."

"O.K. – let's go down to Aunt Meredith's and have a lemonade." Aunt Meredith's at Chelbrough was the Tuck Shop.

Just at that moment there was a knock at the door and Rowland beamed in confidently with his new much-discussed friend just behind him, "Here's Ronald" he said. "Are we too early, Richard?"

"Heavens, no, but I'd just forgotten for a moment you were coming. Look here Harry, I can't come and bathe. "What are you two going to do now?"

"Well, we'll go up to Campbell's room and find John. You'll come up later to tea."

"Of course I will. You two dash off. Enjoy yourselves." And the Chaplain sat down on the humpty-dumpty and Rowland collapsed on the couch with carefree familiarity and his new friend sat rather nervously in the armchair.

CHAPTER FOUR

Peter Campbell turned his pillow over. He used to go and lie down on his bed and think, whenever he could find the time. It generally amounted to about once a week for about half an hour. He took it very seriously and always took lots of clothes off and covered himself over with an eiderdown, however hot the weather.

In a way he had had one piece of luck as a Housemaster. The term before he took over the House, just at the end of the term, there had been what Rattlebones, a senior and traditional Housemaster, had described, with obvious satisfaction, as "a large scale smut row." It had mostly concerned the younger boys and was largely the result of ignorance. The previous Housemaster had relied too much on the scanty instruction given by the preparatory school masters in their leaving lectures and, in this particular case the results had been unholy and puppy-like. About fifteen boys were involved and five of them to such an extent that it was impossible to feel at all easy about them as yet. The former Housemaster had dealt very sensibly and un-sensationally with the boys and no one had been sacked. Peter Campbell always wondered whether any would have been sacked if the new Headmaster, Butler, had been in office then. Nor could he quite make up his mind whether he was lucky that he became Housemaster immediately after the incident, so that he had to deal with the aftermath, but not with the immediate situation; but maybe it would have been better to have dealt with it all from the very beginning. As it was, although he wouldn't have advocated sacking any of the boys, it did relieve him of the official responsibility for not having got them sacked, though of course he would have to take the responsibility of all his subsequent advice and actions. Still, it did allow him a rather freer hand than he would otherwise have allowed himself.

In reality, in spite of a good deal of bluster to the contrary, Peter Campbell didn't really like responsibility on a big scale. It is true that he seldom used to refer anything to do with his House to Butler, the

Headmaster, but this wasn't from any craving for responsibility. He used to say that it was the business of a Housemaster to deal with his own internal problems without dashing off to the Headmaster, unless these problems happened to be ones which concerned the school as a whole. To fortify himself – because instintively he knew that the advice he gave ran quite counter to what Butler would give, and therefore would certainly be considered a school problem by Butler himself – Campbell used to quote the Headmaster's frequent complaints about Housemasters running to him on all occasions about what was purely parochial business. He used to tell himself that he was responsible for the boys under his charge – but then so was old Butler. It was all rather difficult. The parents knew his principles quite well and were always kept closely informed of the advice he was giving their boys. The great majority seemed to have complete confidence in him, and none of them had ever dashed off to the Headmaster for reassurance. In fact, they seemed to prefer, on the whole, that the Headmaster should not become involved. Still, this wouldn't of course satisfy the Headmaster, and Campbell was reasonably certain that, if Butler heard every word of advice given by Campbell to the boys, Butler would look very sincere and very sad and beg Campbell to mend his ways or to depart.

However, Campbell was determined to carry on. He was only just over thirty and he thought he was doing the boys some good. He believed in the advice he gave and, after all, the Headmaster might leave soon and be succeeded by a man who agreed with Campbell's point of view. More than this, Campbell never concealed his attitude at Housemaster's meetings, so it must be generally recognised what kind of advice he gave. Anyway, Campbell's House swore by him and regarded him with spaniel-like loyalty, even though they laughed at some of his studied whimsicalities. Still, Campbell never felt really happy about the whole thing and he was certainly looked upon with some suspicion by the senior masters. The fact that Campbell himself had been a boy at Chelborough and had been taught by many of these same masters, that he was good at most games, intelligent, popular with a lot of Old Chelburians and had a big following both among the athletes and the intellectuals, that too he liked a spot of drink and was enormous fun at a party meant that many of the older masters liked him even though they distrusted his methods and feared his opposition. They were always a little alarmed and nervous about what he would say to the Old Chelburians in those discussions about masters which always spring up among such gatherings. They were also fairly certain that from time to time such discussions did spring up, unsuppressed, if not actually encouraged by Campbell himself, particularly among his beloved, pampered historians, in the happy-go-lucky atmosphere of Campbell's room. Peter Campbell had a wicked tongue and it often spoke without much second thought.

However, Peter Campbell's mind was not moving along these lines as he lay on his bed. It often did, but this hot afternoon was not one of those occasions. Peter was thinking about part of the aftermath of the "large scale smut row". The sun was now shining full into his bedroom and his shaving mirror was throwing an extraordinary shadow onto the table. Surely a round object shouldn't throw a shadow like that? I wish someone had taught me physics sensibly, or isn't it physics? And his mind wandered back again to Reggie and Alex, both in his House. They were about seventeen: Alex looked younger but was actually a little older than Reggie. Both of them had been concerned in the "smut row" and in the many discussions they had had with him, they had been ninety per cent honest and frank. There was no doubt at all that they were really fond of each other, an affection which had lasted now for well over nine months.

Peter really believed that almost all boys, somewhere between the age of twelve and twenty, at one time or another feel a real affection for some other boy, generally of approximately their own age. The degree of this affection varied according to the emotional nature of the boy, and so did the degree of expression of affection which the boy demanded. Some boys desired and strove just for the company of the other boy, some would like to walk arm in arm but would never conceive of holding hands, for some holding hands was not enough and they imagined, in the boring moments of some lessons, romantic kissing and embracing. Campbell believed that to attempt to suppress this affection when it developed was likely to retard the process of outgrowing it. He felt that when boys came to ask him about the appearance of this young emotion the best thing to do was to explain the whole thing to them, to assure them that such emotion was very usual and to tell them not to worry about it. It might take them a month or a year or two years to grow naturally out of it into a capacity for affection for girls. Judging from the very great number of cases he had dealt with, both as a Housemaster and before he had become a Housemaster, Peter Campbell was convinced that his diagnosis was right, though he was never certain that the advice he gave was equally right. It is so difficult ever to be certain about advice.

He never found the senior boy in such relationships with young good-looking boy a difficult problem to deal with. Nine times out of ten it merely meant that the older boy had outgrown the monastic school and was more than ready for a plunge into the exciting whirlwind of mixed society. The far more frequent cases of real affection between boys of the same age presented more difficulties. Frequently the difficulty arose from the difference between the two boys' emotional content, the one desiring much more expression of affection than the other, with the resultant shock, mental disappointment and occasional feeling of disgust and repulsion on the part of the less emotional. Then followed the break, the heart-burning, the belief that if only the whole thing could start again it would be different this time: the frustration, the jealousy, the loneliness, the tears and the slightly sick feeling as one eats the little food one can get down.

But this wasn't really quite one of those cases. If anything Alex was more attached to Reggie than vice versa, yet it was Reggie who, from time to time was in despair. He used to come sadly into Campbell's room about twice a term and ask if he could have ten minutes chat. It was always the same. Alex had lost all interest and was behaving bloodily. Alex went out of his way to avoid him and then, all of a sudden, was delightful and very friendly for a whole afternoon, and the next day he was bloody again. Alex didn't seem to want to go to concerts or the flicks with him. Whereas before he used to suggest all sorts of ways of shaking off unwanted hangers on, now he only really seems to want to shake me off. And then, three weeks later, Reggie would be radiant and Alex and he were to be seen everywhere together. At the moment Reggie was clearly miserable and he was sure to be in again in a day or two for a ten minute chat. Alex was, of course, tiresome; he was behaving like a petulant schoolgirl and deliberately playing with Reggie's affections. Odd really because he is the more attached of the two. The only expression they seem to need is that their friendship should be generally recognised, and it satisfies them just to be seen about everywhere together. Both pairs are proud of their friendship, and for Alex and Reggie there must be constant private expression.

The sun had gone in behind great swollen clouds. It was hotter than ever. Campbell threw back his eiderdown. Well, either way I shall have to get hold of Alex and tell him to stop behaving like a performing seal and then I think I'll have them both in together. I know what. I will ask Dickie and John if they mind my quoting their friendship's tale to Alex and Reggie. In some ways it was harder to deal with because, although Dickie was in my House, John wasn't, and that always led to complications. I shall never forget that evening a year ago, at the friendship's crisis, when John came up and lay on my couch and said he was about to run away, and after a long talk I sent him off to walk round the Little Cricket Field and promised I'd send Dickie down to join him. It took me some time to persuade Dickie to go down, and John told me afterwards that Dickie was pretty dumb when he did turn up. However Dickie didn't come back till nearly midnight and, after that, the friendship continued, gradually simmering down till it assumed ordinary but loyal proportions.

Dickie was now head of Campbell's House and Campbell had no doubt that he would willingly agree. Campbell was fairly certain that John would agree too. It's difficult to get boys in this state to take things seriously, but not too seriously. One can't laugh it off, however much one is tempted to do so, because for Alex and Reggie it's no laughing matter. One thing one can do in these cases is to show the boys the responsibility or consciously allow someone to build up their affections on them, and that's a lesson which, if they learn it, will stand them in good stead.

It's time that Reggie and Alex began to see the whole thing in perspective. If I get hold of them together and tell them the story of Dickie and John and show them that, though Dickie and John are still great friends, they are no longer inseparable and don't spend every idle moment thinking where the other is and what he is doing, then Alex and

Reggie are more likely gradually to see the thing in better perspective. I must paint the original picture or John's and Dickie's affection a little stronger than it actually was, then it will help to convince Alex and Reggie that there is nothing phenomenal, ultra-romantic or quite exceptional about their own case. Well, I'd better just ask the Chaplain about it all first. Richard doesn't know Reggie, but he knows Alex pretty well. Funny how everyone likes Alex, though I don't think he's particularly attractive. I suppose it's that bundle of black hair which flops so oddly about, and it's partly his perky self-assurance. Even old Rattlebones has rather a soft spot for him. Of course it might be easier if I could take a completely detached point of view, but I can't. Reggie and Alex are quite aware that I like them, and nothing can hide it from them. I always wonder to what extent they and the others take advantage of this. On the other hand, boys over sixteen simply won't pay much attention to what one says unless they feel that you like them or are at any rate sympathetic. I remember so well what Bill said to me about a year ago about his Housemaster: "Of course, old Watson talks almost entirely nonsense, but the fact that he is so obviously fond of me and the House makes one want to do what he says, on the whole."

Campbell flicked the green eiderdown finally off. He got up and, as he was putting his trousers on, he suddenly remembered he'd got no biscuits. I shall be drinking beer without doubt, so Alex and Reggie must have something. I could give them tea, but I haven't got any milk. The door of his sitting-room was closed. He stopped and listened. John was obviously no longer alone. Yes, Michael and Harry are both in there chatting away. I'll just go in and say "Hey ho". No, they seem to be involved in a terrific argument and if I go in they'll want to know my opinion, So Peter Campbell tiptoed away and down the stairs, off to the cricket field.

CHAPTER FIVE

As a matter of fact John and Michael and Harry were not in the middle of any literary, philosophical or religious discussion. As Peter Campbell tiptoed away they were merely discussing House affairs. John had picked up some of those Remove essays and had begun reading them. He could remember so well writing on that subject himself a year and a half ago, when he was in the Remove. Campbell had read the poem – one of W H Auden's *Songs out of Another Time*.

> *The stars are not wanted now; put out every one,*
> *Pack up the Moon and dismantle the sun."*

John got off the divan. He had taken off his shoes and he paddled across to the bookcase in his socks. The sort of thing one ought to read on an afternoon like this is a *Horizon* magazine, but I imagine all the good ones are out on loan. No, here's one lying under these papers. At least I think it is. Yes. It was the one with Arthur Koestler's article on the *Yogi and the Commissar* in it. At the moment this was very fashionable among Chelborough's historian "intellectuals". John thought it awfully good though he hadn't really understood it when Campbell had read it aloud in school, especially that bit about the umbilical cord. Anyway, what is an umbilical cord? I remember Campbell telling us, but I've forgotten. I'll look it up. Where's a dictionary? And he found one and fluttered through the pages. Oh, so that's it. Just as well to know before one starts reading. John was in the middle of reading the article when Michael and Harry bounced in.

"Richard has more or less turned us out because he's got Rowland and Ronald, who've booked a kind of date with him. So we've come to dig you out."

"All right, well; what shall we do? It's hardly worth dashing anywhere before tea, and we're going to have tea up here, aren't we? Anyway, the only thing there really to do is to go and watch the cricket." John lay down on the divan again and fiddled with his toes. *Horizon* was balancing dangerously on the edge of Cleopatra. Harry came over and sat on the divan too.

"Push over, John. Anyway it's really cooler here than anywhere else." Harry was wearing a cricket shirt, dark blue shorts and a pair of gym shoes. So was Michael, except that Michael was in the process of taking off his rather dirty cricket shirt. Michael slapped his bare stomach with satisfaction and sat down in the armchair.

John picked up *Horizon* and started reading aloud.

"Oh, Koestler again," Harry said. "Really Campbell's quite mad about Koestler. He's absolutely off Maritain now. He never refers to him at all, and, if anyone mentions him, he just says Fascist and stares out of the window. Campbell has a rather stupid way of just labelling anyone, whom he doesn't like, a Fascist, though he always warns us not to apply labels."

Michael had his eyes shut but he opened them to speak. He was too late. John was already in action.

"Still, Koestler is good you know. I only wish I could remember it properly. Campbell always says 'don't remember it, absorb it', but he never tells us how to absorb it without remembering it."

"Of course", said Harry, " Campbell often talks a lot of rot. I mean, seriously, he does. I don't mean when he talks nonsense on purpose but when he really thinks he's talking sense. For instance, do you remember when we were in the Remove how he used to scoff at scientists and mathematicians? He used to say that all they could do was to 'chase truth with a toothpick'. Now that he's become a Koestler fan his whole attitude has changed. 'You'll never be a good historian unless you keep in touch with the latest mathematics and science'. 'My dear children, the trouble with all of you is that you don't know any biology or you wouldn't write such presumptuous drivel'. Really Campbell is almost as much the victim of his latest intellectual as Alex or Peter is of their latest film star."

"But you're a professional rebel anyway, Michael. Harry leant back on John, and John pushed him away. It was too hot. "And I believe that's really why Campbell likes you so much. You never agree with him. It pays to disagree with him, though I must admit that it hasn't paid me, but really I suppose it's because I mostly agree with him, except of course over his generally agnostic approach to everything. If only he had just a touch of Richard's faith and a few of Richard's angels he'd be marvellous."

Michael liked Campbell but he far preferred Richard. Michael really existed on faith. He had faith abundant, and his faith allowed him to do almost anything he wanted. It certainly didn't insist on very much work in school nor did it insist on his holding the same opinion for very long. He was volatile on principle.

"I'm quite sure Campbell's right over one thing", said Harry, "that things would be far better at Chelborough if the historians were more tolerant of the scientists and the mathematicians of the classics. He's right, too, when he says that if the sixths were properly organised we could all learn a lot from each. Campbell says that we all ought to do elementary philosophy together – all the sixths – and I think, it would be a damned good idea."

"Well, I think it would be a damned sight better, if we did anything as a group, for it to be religion. And, whatever you may say, in many ways Campbell is as much responsible for the isolationism among the sixths as anyone. Most of the other sixths hate us." Michael loved attacking Campbell. It irritated John so much, but in fact there was a great deal in what he said. As no one said anything, he went on, encouraged by his apparent triumph.

"Actually the only person who really provides anything like common ground between the various sixths is Richard."

"I don't altogether agree," said John. "I mean I do agree about Richard, but somehow the people in Campbell's House – I mean the sixth form boys of all kinds – do seem to have a common ground and Campbell's House is stiff with people in the sixth."

"Well, of course, it's easy in Campbell's House." Michael was at it again. "Most of them are musical as well, and they all read the moderns and then they act and all that."

"Anyway I, for one, bloody well wish I was in Campbell's House." John lay back again on Cleopatra. Harry by this time had got on to the window ledge and his legs were dangling out of the window.

"Good God, no," he said. "Personally, I wouldn't swop Herriotts for Campbell's House if I was paid."

"Well, I'd swop old Franklin for Campbell tomorrow if I had the chance. It's all very well for Michael and you, Harry. You're together in Herriott's, but I'm all alone in my House and I often feel very all alone, and it's very different. It isn't possible for anyone to be all alone in Campbell's, unless from choice, and the boy would soon not want to be. Look how Alex blossomed out."

"I wouldn't; I wouldn't be in Campbell's House if I was paid." Michael was by now firmly established in the armchair. One leg was dangling over the arm of the chair. "It's all really too heartily friendly and he seems to know everything that everyone's thinking, quite apart from what they are doing. I think all this free and easy discipline is so much window dressing. After all, we tried it in Herriot's and it simply doesn't work."

"Perhaps that's because Campbell isn't there to bless it."

"Nonsense; – I am right aren't I, Harry?"

"I don't know really, but I agree I wouldn't be in Campbell's House."

"Well, the boys in Campbell's House seem to like it all right. You can't deny that. Anyway, you're jealous, Michael."

"Nonsense. It's a sort of tradition, that's all it is. It's a sort of religion in Campbell's House to enjoy it. They make a fetish of enjoying it and treat Campbell as though he was a kind of Archangel."

"Well, most boys at Chelborough, if they were really honest, would admit they'd like to be in Campbell's. House Oh, hell! I'm fed up with all this." "What about tea? Surely it's tea-time?"

CHAPTER SIX

Butler, the Headmaster, had had a really tiring, fiddling day. His house was some way from the main school buildings and he was having a cup of coffee after dinner. His wife had gone upstairs to pull the curtains at the top of the House. People were apt to turn on the passage lights and they showed out at the top. A warden had been round and warned them once, and Butler was determined it shouldn't happen again.

I wonder why the parents of new boys insist on coming to see me, even though they haven't really anything to ask that they couldn't ask the Housemaster. There had been several of them today. Some of them had explained that "they purposely hadn't troubled me on the first day of the term as they knew I'd be so busy." Why should they think I'm less busy now? I suppose they imagine that I have a half holiday on Saturdays, like everyone else. But that's my trouble; I seem to be the only person at Chelborough who doesn't ever get a half-holiday.

The parents thought Butler quite charming. Most of the boys couldn't quite make up their mind. None disliked him; he wasn't really positive enough to dislike, but although he was always pleasant to them, he seemed to be holding something back, as though he was a little nervous for his dignity.

Butler was nearing fifty. Five years before he had married a girl in her early twenties. She had been a schoolmistress somewhere or other. She adored Butler and was absolutely dominated by him, a kind of keen backbencher in the Headmaster's life. Fortunately this meant she took no part in the school politics. Butler had no children – a pity. Butler got up. Well, I suppose I'd better go and write some letters. I shall have to write three or four at least. The telephone rang and he went over gloomily to answer it.

It was Housemaster Watson. He wanted to come up to see the Headmaster. Butler looked at the clock. It was nearly nine. "Well, Watson, it's a bit late, and I've had rather a tiring day. I've got some letters to write and the Bishop of Bath and Wells is going to be upon me all day tomorrow. But still, if it's important, do come."

Apparently Watson did think it was important and he said he'd be along in about ten minutes. That's rather a nuisance. There isn't much point in shutting up one's office down at the School at seven in the evening, if people are going to chase one over to one's house. That's the trouble, really. I'm the only person here who gets no privacy – never gets a moment to myself but still, fortunately not many people come up after dinner.

Butler walked over and looked at himself in the mirror. He put his tie straight, though, in fact, it was quite straight already. Butler was a tallish man, with thinning well-controlled sandy hair. He had an equally well-disciplined small sandy moustache. Many people create their moustache with forefinger and thumb, but Butler never did this. His moustache had a kind of virginity which could not be publicly molested. There was no doubt that he was quite good-looking and he was always rather consciously dressed. People never knew quite how he managed to keep so spruce in wartime. Butler bicycled everywhere, sitting bolt upright. Sometimes he wore city clothes and looked quite absurd on his bicycle; sometimes he wore vaguely country clothes, but he never looked completely at ease in those either.

The bell rang, and Butler went to open the front door himself. He smiled at Watson. Butler never used his eyes to smile with. He just smiled with his mouth.

"Come in Watson, do. I hope you haven't leaned your bicycle against my roses."

"Oh no, Headmaster, no. I was careful to put it against the garage wall."

"No. I didn't really imagine you would. Only some of the young fry are rather casual and careless. Come in.. No, no. after you."

Inside Butler's study Housemaster Watson sat down in the armchair. Butler had already sat down on the green leather fender seat. Before he had become Headmaster, one of the governors had told him that it was important to see to it that, in any interview, one held the commanding position. Butler remembered this. In fact, Butler remembered almost everything. He was not a professional schoolmaster. His appointment from the Colonial Civil Service to Chelborough had surprised him almost as much as it had a lot of other people.

On the table, near the window there was a whisky decanter and one glass. Butler noticed Watson's eyes drifting towards it. "Have a whisky, Watson?"

"No, I don't think I will, Headmaster, if you don't mind." Watson rather wished there had been two glasses, but Butler didn't seem to notice the omission.

"Well, I'm sorry to trouble you, Headmaster, at this time of night, but I'm very worried over Rowland Brittain and I feel I have got to take a really firm line pretty soon – and I wanted your advice. You know about his family, don't you? Nasty business, really, but it does make me feel rather more than normally responsible for him. You see, his mother is quite incapable of looking after him, and he has no healthy home-life. In fact, as far as it exists at all, it's rather unhealthy. Too much drink, I'm afraid, to be quite frank."

Butler got up and sat in the other armchair. He had decided that he was in for a longish Watson interview and probably dignity wouldn't be an important factor.

"Yes, quite," he said.

"Well, young Brittain is taking his School Certificate this term and it is absolutely vital he should get it, but it is proving very difficult to get him to settle down to work. He's a gregarious little brute and has lots of friends in various Houses. To be frank, I think he's quite sound, but it worries me from the point of view of his work. Well, I decided at the beginning of this term that in the interests of his work I must put a stop to it. As you know, Headmaster, I'm not one to discourage friendships. I believe that, within reason – always remembering of course that one is, so to speak, in loco parentis – a boy should choose his own friends, but in this case I felt that I owed it to the boy to interfere, so I told him at the beginning of the term that I'd rather he saw as little as possible of people in other Houses."

"Yes, quite," said Butler.

Watson was about fifty and a bachelor. He had been a goodish athlete in his day and was a superbly conscientious Housemaster. He always had his half-term reports in well before time and he wrote to all the parents religiously, even if without much life except, of course, when the boy left, and then he wrote with some relief and deliberate emotion. He smelt very clean; he loved washing his hands and always took some time brushing his hair, although there wasn't very much of it nowadays. Tonight he was feeling the heat and he took out a handkerchief and mopped his forehead. "I think I'll change my mind Headmaster, and have a whiskey, if you don't mind.'

Butler poured a moderate whiskey into the lonely glass.

"Water, Watson? I'm afraid we've no soda."

Since Butler obviously wasn't going to say anything as yet, Watson took a gulp and went on. That was better. Watson liked a drink. He leaned back in the chair for the first time and then leaned forward again.

"Well, to cut it short, Headmaster, I'm rather worried about the Chaplain. I can't get him altogether to co-operate. In fact, to be frank, I can't really get him to co-operate at all."

Watson paused. Butler still said nothing. This rather perturbed Watson. Still, he went on.

"The Chaplain came up to see me in my room last night apparently to discuss Rowland Brittain. I couldn't get him to see the point. He said he thought Brittain was miserable and that he'd never get his certificate if he went moping about like this. He seemed to think he needed what he described as the stimulation of friendship. I couldn't agree with him and, though I was perfectly friendly and did my best to see his point of view. I think I made myself pretty plain. However, he didn't agree. Still, we parted very good friends."

"Yes?"

"Well, the story doesn't end there, I'm afraid, Headmaster. Today I learned that young Brittain had missed his extra-tuition. Well, I sent for Brittain to find out where he'd been and I'm afraid it proved to be worse than I thought. Not only had he missed his extra-tuition, but he'd also cut his game. He'd gone up to the Chaplain's room after lunch with young Sharp – you know, the one in Herriot's House – and stayed there the whole afternoon. He even cut House-tea, I'm sorry to say."

Watson paused again. Surely Butler would give him some encouragement at this stage; but Butler only smiled and rubbed his knee. This was rather an irritating habit of Butler's, this knee-rubbing. Watson had often been annoyed by it on similar occasions before. Not quite sure of his ground, Watson carried on resolutely.

"Well, the point is I've got to do something about it. The Chaplain should know quite well what I think. It was only last night that we had that chat. It seems to me he's going out of his way to go against my wishes. After all, I am finally responsible for the boy and he is not. Now, am I to forbid the boy to go and see the Chaplain or am I to forbid the Chaplain to have the boy to his room? It seems to me I've got to do one or the other, though I don't really want to; but I didn't want to do either without asking you, Headmaster. And it's a decision I've got to take more or less at once. I can't very well put it off."

Butler leant forward and lit a cigarette. His lighter worked the very first time.

"I do see what you mean exactly, Watson. It's not at all easy. You see, Richard"– Butler always called the livelier masters by their Christian names –Richard looks upon Chelborough not so much as a school as a parish. He feels responsible to every boy here. That in some ways makes the task of the Housemaster much easier and in many ways more difficult. Peter Campbell has argued all this over with me and as you know he is very much in support of Richard. He believes that, although certain difficulties occur, such as this one, Richard's influence is so healthy that the good far outweighs the difficulties, if I may put it like that. Now, to be honest, I am not absolutely certain that Peter is right but, man and boy, he's seen both sides of Chelborough for many years and his opinion cannot be lightly rejected. As well as that, he is a Housemaster himself."

Butler's cigarette had gone out, and he lit it again with equal ease.

"After all, we all say, and I hope we believe it, that the Chapel is the centre of the school life, – and we must remember that Richard has very nearly succeeded in making it that. Of course, you know as well as I do that I don't approve of everything that takes place in the Chapel – but that's another point. One difficulty is that Richard has a very clear view of what he believes is right; and no normal argument will move him. The other difficulty is that there is, so to speak, in Richard a shadow behind every Housemaster's throne. The boy goes, perhaps, to his Housemaster and if he is not satisfied he goes up to the Chaplain and asks his advice without telling Richard what his Housemaster has already said. Now Richard, I'm afraid, rather tends to blunder in. He doesn't always pause to ask whether or not the boy has already discussed the matter with his Housemaster, with the result that Richard sometimes unwittingly gives entirely contrary advice. I genuinely believe that there is no malice in what he does but the results are certainly sometimes confusing to the boy.

"There's more to it than that, I think, Headmaster. Part of the reason why the boys are so anxious and willing to go and consult the Chaplain, and for that matter Campbell, is that those two always give the boys the kind of advice they want to get – often I am afraid only confirming them in their weaknesses. Whereas we others give the advice that we think best, willingly sacrificing popularity as a result. It's easy to be popular with boys if you always tell them what they want to know."

"Yes, I know what you feel, Watson, but I don't think you're being quite fair to Richard or to Peter. I believe, – and especially in Richard's case – that he sincerely believes his advice is right, and he doesn't think it right to withhold the right advice if he is asked for it. I assure you that I am aware of the problem, – the problem of the lively Chaplain in a school; it's difficult for the Housemasters always to co-operate with him or for him to co-operate fully with the Housemasters. Yes, Watson, it's a problem. I had a long talk with Richard early this week. Nobody could have been nicer. He promised me that he sincerely wished to co-operate with the Housemasters and I believe him. You must remember that the excitement of the immediate problem often goes to his head."

"I know, I know, Headmaster; but it is difficult. Somehow he seems to think that school rules don't apply to boys if they are with him, and that in itself creates among the boys suspicion of rules in general. That's unhealthy. It's unhealthy in a school."

Yes, I know that too. But then again I don't believe it's a conscious thing with Richard. I believe that, if he remembers a thing is against the rules, he doesn't allow the boys to do it, but he doesn't always think in terms of rules. And the boys, I suppose, don't generally remind him."

"Yes, I know, Headmaster. But, if you don't mind me saying so, I don't believe you'd feel quite the same if you were a Housemaster."

"Perhaps not, Watson, perhaps not. But to come back to Brittain. In this case I don't think I'd take any action this weekend. Let me have a word with Richard. I'll try to see him sometime tomorrow; then I'll give you a ring and perhaps you might ask him round and have another word with him."

"Thank you very much, Headmaster. Yes, I think that's right. Well, I'd better be going. I'm afraid I've kept you rather long."

Watson got up and moved towards the door. Butler got up too. Watson pulled his coat down from behind and touched the knot of his old Shirburnian tie.

"Don't trouble, Headmaster. I can find my way out easily. It's not quite dark yet."

"Not at all, of course I will."

And Butler walked to the front door with Watson. He opened the door and looked up at the sky.

"Good night, Watson."

"Good night, Headmaster."

Butler waited till Watson was out of the gate, then he shut the front door, went back into his study and picked up his pen to write to his mother.

CHAPTER SEVEN

Watson's short bicycle ride up to the Headmaster's private house had taken him past the windows of Campbell's room. There was a clattering noise coming from it. The windows were open and unrestrained, discordant jazz music was sweeping out into the surroundings. Watson looked up. Campbell is entertaining Old Chelburians and a certain number of boys in his House of all ages, thought Watson to himself. I never understand what good Campbell can think such entertainment does anyone. I suppose he imagines that he gets to know the boys better that way. It's really time he stopped being a Peter Pan and took his responsibilities in a slightly more adult way.

In fact Peter Campbell was not in his room. He had taken the four Old Chelburians into supper in the Masters' Room and had then taken them straight down to the "Old Maid of Perth". He was still there. His room was full of boys of varying ages, rather more than it really should have had on such a hot evening, and there were no Old Chelburians. The boys were in various degrees of attire. Several had had baths and were in pyjamas of strange exotic colours. Some, wore dressing gowns, some didn't. There was a strong smell of toothpaste David and Dickie were in white flannels and had pale pink second eleven scarves casually draped round their necks. David, Dickie, Alex and Reggie were sitting on the divan. They were all prefects in Campbell's House. Michael had gone up to Richard's room, but Harry and John were there, sitting rather uncomfortably back to back on the humpty-dumpty in front of the bookcase. It was very doubtful if they had their respective Housemaster's permission to be away from their Houses. They were idly pulling out some of the obscurer poets and reading little snatches to each other. "This is a good couplet," said John. "Anon wrote it. God, what a lot of good things Anon wrote:"

Christ, that my love were in my arms
And I in my bed again.

Alex leaned forward on the divan and shouted across to Harry. You had to shout when a record was on. "Where's Michael?"

"Oh, he's up with Richard. He wants to see him about some pseudo problem and he wanted to get in before those four O.Cs arrive. When they get back from the 'Old Maid of Perth' with Campbell, they are going to go up to Richard and intend to sleep on his floor. They've really come over for Holy Communion tomorrow. If they go to the seven o'clock one, they can be back by nine for Church parade. Richard is apparently terribly pleased. It's quite cheered him up. He was rather depressed this afternoon. Rather a good show really."

"They rather missed you today, John," David was speaking. "What were you doing?"

"I didn't do any work at all this afternoon, but I thoroughly enjoyed myself. Nobody can work every afternoon of the week. The point is I honestly can't afford to give up two and a half days a week to cricket. And as you know it's almost impossible to work in the evening after an afternoon's cricket in the sun. Cricket's wonderful. It just drains away all your powers of resistance, but all the same it's rather a long process."

"Really, John, you talk more concentrated tripe in a square minute than anyone I know. What are you up to, Harry?"

Harry was by now searching about rather vaguely in a dictionary. He was looking up "pornography".

"Here, John, here's a wonderful word, 'Pornocracy – Pornocratic – a government unduly influenced by harlots.' You could work it into an essay; you're bang in the middle of the eighteenth century aren't you?"

"Yes, I could and by God I will. Don't let me forget it – pornocratic – that's marvellous. Aren't words wonderful, David?"

"I dunno. I prefer girls, anyway." David hated the conversation of the historians.

The young group round the radiogram had been talking about someone whom Rattlebones was going to thrash on Monday, and there had been a good deal of argument whether the whole thing was fair or unfair. Peter Campbell came in. The boys all knew he had been to the "Old Maid of Perth" and looked at him with interest. Except that his orange tie was flopping out he showed no signs of wear or tear.

He looked around, went to the cupboard, took a glass and poured out some beer for himself. Then he went and sat on the arm of a fully occupied armchair. "Isn't anyone drinking any lemon squash?" There was a cry of "There isn't any."

They had switched the wireless on and the pips betrayed the time.

"Good heavens," said Campbell, "It's ten o'clock. Surely all you young miseries are supposed to be in bed at a quarter to ten."

"Oh, but it's Saturday night. What does it matter? Tomorrow's Sunday, sir."

"I don't care a hoot, not a hoot." Campbell looked round triumphantly. No one was either surprised or impressed. "Small boys need sleep. Early to bed, etc., etc. Who the hell is House prefect this fortnight, anyway? You are John, aren't you?"

"No, Campbell. Alex is."

"Well, Alex, you ought to have done something about it. Anyway I can't clear this rabble out. Dickie, you're head of the House; it's traditional for you to clear them out. No one listens to me. Nobody ever tells me anything."

Dickie got up and seized a cricket bat. There was a lazy stir.

"Come on you people, out you get. I'll strike the last person out."

There was no apparent hurry. The first of the non-prefects was by the door, and other boys were picking up glasses off the floor and generally finding any excuse for postponing their departure. The non-prefects had filed away and the room was much quieter.

"You'll have to go soon, Harry and John, won't you? You have to be back in your Houses by quarter-past, don't you?"

"Yes; it is a bloody bore. I really think we're old enough to be treated as though we weren't complete children."

"Oh, I don't know. But, actually, except for casual gradations by quarter of an hour in the time of lights out and a few very small infantile privileges, there isn't really much difference of treatment between boys of thirteen and eighteen. There really ought to be more."

Harry got up and sat on the arm of the chair in which Campbell had been sitting. There was a bit more room now. Campbell was leaning against the mantelpiece with his legs crossed. He poured himself out another beer. Then he moved over to the divan. "Push up, I'm going to abide on Cleopatra. Dickie and Reggie moved up a bit, rather unwillingly, and Campbell plumped himself down.

"Why don't you go and sit on that chair, Campbell. It's terribly hot with five on Cleopatra." Alex looked up brightly.

"Well, I adore Cleopatra and I'm going to sit on her. If you don't like it, Alex, you can go and sit on the chair." Alex didn't move. It was really rather a squash. He and Campbell had a minor fight for one of the cushions and then they settled down.

"Look here. Campbell, what do you think about tomorrow? It's terribly difficult. John Piper's coming down to criticise the exhibition of last term's art products. That's in the afternoon, and Ben Britten and Peter Pears are down to judge the Music and Singing competitions after tea, and I want to go and hear that. I can't possibly miss hearing Michael singing his Irish song. And then isn't Britten coming up here after supper to talk about Auden and some new portentous thing he's writing that's being put to music. Well, I want to go to all of them but I can't possibly spare the time. Which shall I go to? Harry flicked one leg out.

"You must make up your own mind, Harry, Personally I should be rather inclined to reconsider the decision that you can't spare the time to go to all three. You'll probably get much more out of them than you will out of any book you are reading; after all, you can read the book any day."

"Yes, but one could always say that, in which case one would never read any books."

"Well, anyway, I'm sure you and John ought to be going. Get up, John, and buzz off and, for the love of Michael, go back to your Houses and don't go wandering round the courts."

John loped up, pulled his shorts up and he and Harry went off.

"Goodnight, Campbell."

"Goodnight, you two children. Be good."

Campbell was left alone with his prefects. He always rather liked the rare occasions when this happened on a Saturday night. Generally there were some Old Chelburians about, but not tonight. The room seemed rather empty.

"Let's have some tea" said David.

"Well, you can, children, but I think I will stick to beer. I've got some tea but I haven't any milk. You've got some milk, haven't you, Reggie? Go into House and get it and I'll put the kettle on."

And the tea was made and the conversation turned to today's cricket match and then they went on discuss the small boys and the ludicrous play they had put on at the end of last term.

David had moved over to the armchair, almost traditionally sat in by the head of the House, late on Saturday evenings. He was fast asleep. They sat around quietly listening to the gramophone. Campbell sat on the lid and wobbled the knob so that it played very sexily and softly. It finished and Campbell got up and took it off. David got up, too.

"Reggie and Dickie and I, and possibly Alan are going to the eight communion o'clock tomorrow. Shall we pick you up?"

"Yes, do."

"Well, goodnight Campbell."

"Goodnight, Campbell, see you tomorrow"

"Goodnight, children, goodnight."

PART II

ROUGH GRASS

CHAPTER EIGHT

Some weeks had passed and Peter Campbell was in very good form; things were really going very well. True, he looked nervously at the "Killed on Active Service' list in *The Times* first thing after breakfast every morning. Although he didn't actually want to see the names of any of his real friends appear, he was indefinably disappointed if he didn't know anyone at all in the list. Really, in spite of France in 1940 and Dunkirk, it was surprising how few of his real friends had been killed. Most of those who had died had been at school with him and, except for a very few, he had felt no emotional grief and for a small and short duration. What he did dislike was the number of his recent and really close friends, boys whom he had taught and was fond of, who had been taken prisoners of war. He hated that and writing to them. It was easy the first time, but, after that, it was very difficult. There was nothing really to answer in their letters and there was little that happened at Chelborough which wouldn't seem entirely trivial and ludicrous to a prisoner of war. Nowadays the generations changed so quickly that even boys who had only left about eighteen months ago wouldn't know the present highlights. With the boys leaving before they were eighteen, they seemed scarcely to have arrived before they had left. Hardly anyone was a Prefect for more than three terms.

This was one of the things that always annoyed Campbell about Butler and Watson, Rattlebones and the other senior Housemasters. They were always bemoaning the fact that the Prefects no longer seemed capable of showing much trust-worthiness. The prefects, according to Butler and Co, were erratic and unreliable. They seemed to have lost some of the dignity of former days. And, though they never said it in public, Campbell felt fairly certain that they believed it was chiefly the result of his and Richard's influence. They never seemed to realize that these boys were nearly a year younger than the prefects of two years ago and that in normal times a boy was a House prefect three or four terms before he became a School Prefect, whereas now he was often Head of his House and a School Prefect after only one term's apprenticeship. Personally, Campbell thought these boys were doing a marvellous job. There were interminable Home Guard duties, Corps parades, agricultural work, shelter life, and the organisation of all this rested almost entirely on the boys. They were also expected to play games with the same vigour as ever and work just as hard and enthusiastically for their scholarships, even though neither a higher certificate nor a Varsity scholarship would be much good to a dead pilot who had never even seen Magdalen tower. It always surprised Campbell how enthusiastically the boys did work – take John, for example – considering that whatever happened there was no prospect of his going up to the Varsity till after the war. Death, you know, was much with all these boys. They didn't think of it perpetually; in fact there were long periods when it never entered their heads at all, but sometimes before they went to sleep, or when two of them, say Harry and Bill, were talking seriously together about death.

This generation didn't seem to look upon it very heroically. They considered it rather grimly and sadly. For most of them, of course, it was still more of an intellectual problem. I suppose that's because no one has yet been killed whom they really know, no boy who has left recently. It has always been uncles or friends of father. In some cases, of course, it had been father, but never someone of their own age and ideas. But that won't last, Campbell thought. The R.A.F. are putting people into the air very quickly now. The real shock can't be long delayed. Still, Watson was wrong when he kept on saying how lucky these boys were to be at Chelborough where, to all intents and purposes, things mostly went on fairly normally. The atmosphere was not a normal one for schoolboys. For one thing their masters were mainly old. I think it's partly because the boys feel so often the probable shortness of their lives. I think that's why many of them seem so desperately anxious to retain and cling to a kind of childish freshness, which Watson and Co. enjoy calling irresponsibility. Campbell was drowsy. He had dropped into the Masters' room after dinner to see if three were any notes for him and had picked up The Times, but now it was lying slightly crumpled on his knees. He hadn't glanced at it for at least five minutes. Oh, hell. I must go up to my room.

Still, I mustn't complain. I'm lucky to be considered indispensable here and so I don't have to go to this bloody war. There's a great deal of the coward in me. Two masters, Ralph and Herbert both went, even though they were equally indispensable; still, on the whole people haven't gone dashing wildly off, as they seem to have done last time, and there are still quite a few men here who are much younger than me. That eases my conscience a bit. I wonder what their consciences are like.

What have I got to do tonight? Oh yes, I ought to see. Richard and I suppose Alan later, but if I see Alan, I shan't have time to correct those essays properly as well as going to see Richard, and I'm determined to see Richard. He seemed to be terribly depressed and out of form at supper tonight. Wasn't that cold meat ghastly? When Percy pulled Richard's leg a bit about his papist prayers and Saint Paul, Richard really seemed quite annoyed, whereas generally he loves being ribbed and reacts with grand, illogical vigour. It's a pity Percy's married and doesn't come into supper more often. Yes, I must certainly go and pay Richard a visit later on. I'll go and give him a ring. Campbell wandered over to the telephone. It had only been put into the Masters' room a year or two ago. Campbell hated the telephone. It was too impersonal; it was so difficult to detect the mood of the person you were talking to. You could never see the answer in the eyes, and how can you talk to a person for long if you can't be sure of the reaction.

"Hello, Richard. This is – well, guess who? Quite right, – how clever you are. Look, I'm coming up to see you later on tonight, so don't say you are going to bed early or anything— no, no, you, can finish confirming all your boys, I shan't be up for hours. – Hey-ho, I'll trickle up later on. No, it's nothing world-shaking; I just thought it would be nice to see you for a change."

Campbell went out of the swing door. He got on the wrong bicycle at first but hadn't gone very far when he noticed that the brakes worked quite well. He turned round and went back to fetch his own. It was only about a five minutes bicycle ride to his House. When he returned to the House, he began talking to Dickie, and Roger – Roger was helping Dickie with his French prose – when Paul appeared to interrupt him.

"Could I come along and see you, sir, for a few minutes?"

"Well, if it is really only for a few minutes, certainly. But, be honest, is it a long or a short one, because if it's a long one, I'd rather put it off till tomorrow evening, unless it's urgent. You see, I've promised to see Richard and Leslie and Alan tonight and I doubt if I shall even have time to see Alan."

"I suppose it is likely to be rather a long one. It's not urgent; tomorrow will do: before or after Prayers, sir?"

"Oh, after. Immediately after."

It was about eleven thirty when Alan left Campbell's room and Campbell went down to bicycle off to Richard. It was a mouldy sort of evening. It would have been better if it had rained today, so that there would have been that fine after-rain smell. He reached the great main block of school buildings in cold grey stone. Chelborough, one of those formless nineteenth century buildings – a big main gate with a nondescript crest over it and a pokey little porter's lodge on the right as you went in. Then there was three-sided cold grey court with classrooms on the ground floor and masters' rooms above. Porter's Court it was called. How dead a school building is without the boys or the sound of boys. It's like going back into an empty cinema to look for an umbrella.

Richard's rooms were in Porter's Court and Campbell went up the staircase. He knocked at the door and, as there was no answer, went in. He wasn't surprised at the lack of an answer because Richard seldom said "Come in" but he was surprised to find no one there. The light was on. He had seen the light from downstairs. Richard's black-out was never very good, and he was constantly arguing with the wardens whether the black-out was supposed to be directed against aeroplanes or submarines. Finally, in self-protection, Richard had been forced to join the ranks of the wardens himself. A plug pulled nearby. That's where he is, of course! I might have guessed. I wonder if it's Richard's South American bug that prods him along to the lavatory so often. I must ask him. Richard came in.

"Hullo. Peter. I'm glad you've come. I thought you would be later than this. I've just shot Sebastian out. He's a good man. Should be a god-send to old Rattlebones' House in a year's time."

"Good heavens, old Rattlebones will have had a fit at your keeping Sebastian all this time."

"Oh, no, that's all right. I suddenly remembered at quarter to eleven and rang him up. He was frightfully nice and said I could keep him as long as I like. In fact he said he'd rather I had one long talk with Sebastian than several short ones."

"A bit two-edged I call that, but I suppose that didn't occur to you, Richard?"

"No, it didn't. I don't really believe it was. I honestly believe the old man was trying to be quite helpful, for once. I must say he did add that it would be better in future if I rang up before quarter past ten instead of long after."

"You're a credulous old Christian, Richard. I suppose you don't realize that Rattlebones has made a note of the whole thing and, sooner or later, when the right moment comes, he'll quote it and a lot else, to Butler."

"Oh, I don't know. I can't really be bothered. As a matter of fact, Peter, I've had a lot of trouble the last day or two with Brancker."

"Over one of his boys, I suppose?"

"Yes, – Philip. You see, Philip is desperately keen to act in the School play next term – you know "Rope". He said both Brancker and Miles thought he hadn't got the time to spare if he was to get his languages scholarship next year. Well, I must say, I felt they were putting things rather grimly. Can't act this year because of a scholarship exam next year!"

"Well, what did you say, Richard?"

"At first I sort of hedged a little. I told Philip he did have rather a lot of outside activities for a scholarship boy. And he, of course, quoted your historians back to me and said that they were allowed to act and all that. I told him if out of school activities were taking up too much of his time, he must give up something. I suggested the Choral Society or the Glee Club; both of which are time-consuming. But I added that perhaps the play was the best to sacrifice because it was chiefly for personal reasons that he wanted to act in it, whereas the other things were more corporate shows. I said I didn't think his Housemaster would mind as long as he gave something up.

"Well, I suppose it didn't turn out like that."

"No. not exactly. That ass Philip went along to old Brancker and told him what I'd said, I didn't mind that really, except that I'm sure Philip was pretty blunt about it. According to Philip, Brancker said he was sorry Philip hadn't accepted his advice and had thought fit to go to someone else for further consultation. He must have been pretty wild to say that and then he told Philip that he thought he was better able to judge and that he's already told the authorities that Philip couldn't act and that was that. Then Brancker rang me up and I went along. He was in an absolute riot of rage. He asked me to refrain from giving advice to any of his boys without previous consultation."

"But that's ludicrous. I mean to say. One..."

"Oh well, I gradually convinced him that that was absurd. You see, the trouble was that it was nothing really to do with the scholarship at all. The whole thing was a kind of plot arranged by Brancker. He thinks Philip is a weak, easily-led character; he doesn't approve of the other boys who are acting in the play and doesn't want Philip to associate with them, – mostly your historians, as a matter of fact! That's the real point; but he did add that Philip was due to act a girl's part and he thought that very unhealthy for a boy like Philip— whatever that may mean."

"Yes, I know, I know. There's really nothing one can do with people like Brancker." Campbell was thoroughly interested. He really quite enjoyed these kind of rows, though he far preferred not to be involved in them himself. He would have found it very dull in a school which had no Watsons, Rattlebones's and Branckers.

"Well, that's not the end. Today I got a letter from Philip's father – a retired Indian Army Colonel. He said, more or less, that he'd be glad if I would discourage Philip from coming up to my room. He knew that I had had a lot of influence over him in the past and he was very grateful to me for it, but now that Philip's scholarship was in the near future he felt that any distractions must be avoided. I nearly fell flat. Obviously, old Brancker put him up to it. I went and taxed Brancker with it before supper and he said he hadn't. He'd just written to Colonel Robertson and told him he thought the boy ought to concentrate entirely on his work."

"I simply don't believe it. No parent would write off like that unprompted. It's a bloody scandal. Did his Pa write to Philip too?" Campbell got up and fetched an ashtray.

"Yes, he wrote to him too – on much those same lines. I must try to get hold of the father, but he's not coming down on Governors Day, – not till much later on. It really leaves one in an absurd position. I must go and see Butler."

"Probably that's exactly what Brancker wants you to do. I should think it over. If you go dashing off, it will save Brancker the trouble of bringing it to Butler's attention himself."

"Well, there's nothing to bring. It's absurd."

"Oh, I don't know."

"That's nonsense, Peter. Either I was right or I was wrong."

"My dear Richard – you are childish. It isn't a question of right or wrong. So much depends on the presentation, so much on the innuendos."

"No, that's absurd. No, I must see Butler. And then I've had this trouble with Watson over Rowland. You know two or three Saturdays ago he came up here and never told me he'd got all sorts of other things to do and he cut all sorts of extraordinary things; now Butler's gone and made it almost impossible for him to come up here at all. At least the boy has great upheaving pangs of conscience if he does. So I've more or less had to discourage him from coming myself – which is all very sad."

"So things aren't going very well, Richard? No wonder you're a bit depressed."

"Depressed? Good heavens, no. I'm not depressed, though I did feel rather jaded after that quarrel with Butler over the servants' salaries, It's practically sweated labour, you know."

Campbell tried to cheer Richard up, but it was a difficult task as Richard was convinced he was perfectly cheerful. Campbell discussed his House with Richard – whether to make Alex or Reggie head next term. It was rather a pointless discussion as Campbell had already made up his mind to choose Reggie, but he hoped the Chaplain would agree. Richard didn't. He wasn't decisive, but he seemed to think Alex. Richard suggested putting on another kettle.

"Don't bother," said Campbell. "I really must go and tuck myself up. It's awfully late and I suppose you've got to be up before dawn again tomorrow, Richard?"

"Well, not before dawn, but quite early."

"What saint are we praying for tomorrow?"

"My dear Peter, how many times have I told you we don't pray for saints; they pray for us. If you must know, it's St. John tomorrow."

"Well, it's nice to know someone's taking the trouble up there to pray for us. Do they pray for me?"

"Of course they do – and if you're going to say it's an awful waste of time you won't annoy me."

"Oh well, in that case I'll go," and Campbell went off.

What a tiresome time Richard has. At last someone seems to have succeeded in getting him down. Still, there's no point in my being patronising. I expect it will be my turn next.

CHAPTER NINE

Wednesday was wet. There were little intermittent gaps in the rain, but never long enough for them to be noticed or appreciated. It was one of those days when one lost, early on, all interest in the weather. Most people would have sworn, quite wrongly, that it had been raining all day. The Corps parade had been miserable. The boys, who took these parades rather more seriously in war-time, had been lethargic and uninterested. It was unlucky that this particular Wednesday should have been scheduled for the Company in defence. That had involved a good deal of lying about, and the boys had concentrated on choosing their positions more for the protection they gave from the rain than from the enemy. When Campbell had criticised one particularly glaring example of sheltering under trees, the section commander apologised, explaining that perhaps he had been thinking too much of hostile aircraft – an ingenious but irritating answer.

Campbell had got very wet. He had felt it his duty to prance about a good deal in the open and to disregard the rain. The drops had begun eventually to trickle down his neck – there is no defence against this particular form of infiltration – and, worse than that, his battledress had begun to smell like a wet dog. Campbell hated that particular smell. Back in his own room, several cups of tea had more or less restored his spirits. He would have felt better if he'd been able to have a bath, but there was no hot water on Wednesdays.

There was one blessing, however; he hadn't got to go into school for first lesson. I think I'll have a pipe – Campbell very seldom smoked a pipe, although there were always masses of them cluttered about his room. Campbell wasn't really annoyed when Harry came in. He rather wanted company.

"Hallo, aren't you in School?"

"No, we've got a study period. I simply can't understand this book, so I nipped on my bike and came over."

Campbell looked at the book – Collingwood's *New Leviathan*.

"Well, Harry, I really think you should be able to understand enough of this to pursue your way to its magnificent end."

Harry shut the book and picked up his notebook which had slipped on to the floor. Campbell didn't want Harry to go; he wanted company.

"By the way," Campbell said. "Have you heard from Bill recently?"

"Yes, as a matter of fact, I have. I got a ludicrous letter yesterday. At least the letter was all right, but there were all sorts of illustrations and hieroglyphics all over the envelope. I've got it here.

Harry dived into his inner pockets and pulled out a wallet and a pile of letters. Boys have little respect for their pockets or the shapes of their suits. Bill had left six months before to go into the R.A.F. and, although he was nine months older than Harry, they had been tremendous friends. He was one of those boys who occur once every so often at a school. He was clever, had sat for a history scholarship at Cambridge and was a really brilliant athlete. Every game came to him with equal ease. The only games at which he was not first-class were those he seldom played, such as golf. Not content with distributing these gifts, the powers that be had almost seemed to overdo it, for Bill was superbly good looking in an entirely masculine way. He had great broad shoulders, strong hips and sturdy legs and a face that paled and sunburned with equal charm. If Bill looked serious, and he loved to look serious, it was impossible not to like him. If his face puckered up into a riot of smiles, that was the end. His eyes, when they were at rest, were blue and his hair was rough and a kind of mouse colour. One never really noticed the fact that it was curly.

Bill was quite aware of the blessings he had received from above. He was consciously and deliberately modest. People who have all the superficial blessings are fools not to be. Although this calculated modesty had in no way deceived Campbell, Bill's own generation and most of the masters had been captivated by it. Practically no one was jealous of Bill and he had hosts of friends, none of whose admiration and reverence was in any way shaken by Bill's changing affections. He was a specialist in friendship and adored the role of confidant. Very often, when some boy or other had finally confided in him, he rather lost interest though never enough to release the boy from the ties of affection.

Both Campbell and Bill were well aware of these little flaws and Bill never tried to hide them from Campbell. Campbell hated the way that Bill allowed others to fall under his spell. Bill despised much of the shallowness in Campbell. In a way they had been rivals, although their fields were quite different. It was a technical rivalry which both of them sensed, and it was a rivalry which could never diminish because there was no way of playing it out. Very few people at Chelborough really knew Bill, but Campbell did. Practically no one knew Campbell, but Bill did. Bill and Campbell were very firm friends.

Harry worshipped Bill and Bill was very fond of Harry. Harry had the advantage of being Bill's last friend before When Bill left Chelborough, he was now without present rivals. He threw Bill's letter over to Campbell.

"Read it straight away, Campbell. You see I want to answer it tonight."

Campbell sorted out the pages, which were in the wrong order and began to read:

"Harry". It began. It was the custom for this particular group to begin their letters without a prefix and always to end them "Hey-ho – love." It saved thought. Part of it they'd acquired from Richard, part from Campbell.

Harry,

I've not written for a long time. Shame on me. Anyway, I expect you've been pretty busy one way and another – especially with your scholarship. How's it going? I don't suppose you've even had time to consider my short space of silence. Look, I'm hoping to get down next Saturday, as this course is supposed to end then, but it all depends on the flying weather, so I can't possibly tell for certain. We may be kept on to finish off our flying hours, or we may be lucky and get a spot of leave.

Don't go and put anything off. I mean, if John or Michael's parents are down and have asked you out to supper, don't go and cancel it or anything. Because, as you know, one can never be certain. I'd hate the weekend to end in a kind of damp squib for you.

Flying? – Yes, I'm getting a bit better, but I don't take to it very easily. I'm a bit more confident now. It's fine by oneself. One can go trotting off exploring. There are the usual rumours floating around – the strongest one is Rhodesia, but I don't know. It's no good boring you by telling you what I'm flying because you don't know one type from another.

Life is much the same from the broader angle; – the time for action gets nearer, but still, thank God, seems a long way off. The end I think is still not quite in sight – possibly next Christmas. I wonder whether peace will bring its hoped-for happiness or whether there'll be reforms and revolutions which will change everything.

How's Campbell? – still entertaining – with all those satellites – Dickie, John, Michael, David, Roger, – God, what a crowd! – but I mustn't be rude. Look don't you go showing this letter to Campbell. It always irritates me the way everyone shows letters to him. Still, I know you wouldn't.

Well, Harry, it's time we got back to you. How are you? Good form? Got old Herriot taped? When am I going to see you again? – Soon, I hope – I mean if this Saturday doesn't come off. If it doesn't, I'll do a pop-along as soon as I can.

It's time I stopped – this is probably unbearably disjointed, boring and unreadable. I'm getting fat again – again? Yes, I got thinner at one point – all right – sorry.

Tell Campbell I'm writing to him. I shan't actually. 'Give my love to you know who and for yourself a double dose.

Hey-ho.

Love.

B.

Campbell handed the letter back to Harry.

"Well, I hope he comes. Has he got to go and stay with Watson, or did he stay there last time?"

"No." Harry picked up the *Daily Express* whilst Campbell had been reading Bill's letter. "He's done both Butler and Watson; he can sleep on Cleopatra this time, which is much more fun."

"You weren't supposed to show me that letter, Harry. In fact you were deliberately instructed not to."

"Oh, no, nor I was. Still, what does it matter? Anyway, you should have stopped me when you got as far as that."

"Yes, I suppose I should really. What a funny person Bill is."

CHAPTER TEN

Today was hot. The Athletic ground was very green. The fact that there had been very little sun this summer had allowed the grass to retain its spring texture and colour. On three sides of the ground there were pine trees, very tall with bald patches under each. On the far side there were massed, unkempt rhododendrons, but they were over now. On half-holiday afternoons it was marvellous to go down and run over the hurdles or round the grass track, either seriously competing against a stop watch or just for fun, – and then to go and bathe and come back to the Athletic ground and lie down there in the sun, and wander across the cricket ground to Aunt Meredith's for a drink, a sticky "yellow", and then up the gravel path, clinking a coin against the iron-railing, back to tea.

Harry had been running against the stop watch and not very successfully. Once again he had done eleven and one-tenth for the hundred yards. It seemed as though he would never do eleven. He was lying away by himself, in the far corner of the ground, chewing one piece of grass and tickling his wrist with another. He hadn't bathed yet, because he was waiting for John. The pine tree was blocking the sun and he wriggled forward a bit so that it could shine full on him. There was just a breath of wind. You could feel it, but it wasn't enough to disturb the leaves.

John's House was in the semi-finals of the relay. It was a medley, two "quarters" and two "two-twenties". Only the winners went forward into the finals. John was a useful quarter miler but he wasn't in proper training. The scheme had been explained to Harry in detail after lunch. Instead of John running last, as would be expected by the opponents, he was going to run first. The plan was for him to gain twenty or thirty yards, which they were sure the sprinters could hold, and then to leave the opposing teams, who were certain to run last, a lot to make up in the last quarter. In this way John thought that the other teams would be rattled, would misjudge the pace, try to make up the ground too quickly and crack-up. If everyone ran true to form John's House couldn't win, but in this way they hoped to steal the race.

The first heat of the relay was about to begin and John's group stopped practising and sat in a little cluster to watch. It wasn't much of a race; it was a procession. Campbell's House won it in a canter, and there was Campbell, looking delighted, surrounded by boys in his House. Campbell never made the least pretence. He never attempted to disguise his delight when his boys did well. There was none of that kind of mild, official pleasure at success which so many Housemasters seem to think it right to adopt. Campbell and Reggie and Alex and Dickie apparently weren't even going to bother to watch the other semi-final. They were wandering off together to the swimming pool. How typical, thought Harry, and rather bloody really, though I don't know why it should be. Why should one watch potential rivals if one doesn't want to? There was some terrific joke on. Another of Campbell's, I suppose; yes, it must be, he's laughing louder than anyone. Harry had a great admiration for Campbell. I don't suppose I'd have done history at all but for him and now here I am a probable scholar.

Harry turned his head. The draw for places was over and John's heat was about to start. The other three competitors were crouched in professional attitudes, with fingers strained. John, of course, was not crouching but standing, slightly bending forward. Why wouldn't he ever do anything the same as anyone else? He always insists on a kind of amateur attitude to games, but that isn't really the reason. It doesn't matter what it is. John always has to be different. It's nonsense really this mania of his that he can't write well unless it is after ten o'clock at night.

They were off. John was soon five yards ahead and, by the back straight, he was a good fifteen yards clear. Harry stood up so that he could see better. Hallo, something's gone wrong, the others are catching him. It looks as though he has misjudged things himself. It was true; they were catching him and they continued to do so. Eventually a very tired John handed over the baton, not with the planned twenty yards lead, but with a mere five. John flung himself on the ground. My God, he'll be angry, though he'll pretend, of course, that he doesn't care. The other three members of John's team struggled hopelessly. By the time the last quarter began their lead had vanished to two yards and their last string soon tailed off.

Harry, still sitting away on the edge of the ground, waited for John to come over to him. Harry's thoughts turned to Bill, as they generally did in vacant moments like these, and he went over in his mind in a leapfrog way the incidents of Bill's visit last weekend. It had been quietly marvellous. Bill had arrived late on Saturday. Harry always consciously used the name Bill in his thoughts; somehow it made the whole reminiscence more personal and possessive. Bill had gone straight up to Campbell's room and dumped that absurd little brown suitcase and blue-grey haversack. Then he'd come up to Herriot's to find Harry, and they'd both been self-consciously shy and indifferent and casual, but neither had really been able to disguise in their eyes the excitement of the meeting. Bill looked terrific in his air force uniform.

"I'm just going to nip into supper with Campbell but I've said I won't go down to the hoary 'Old Maid of Perth' with him. Harold, Rusty and Charlie are all down for the night and they are joining us at the 'Old Maid', but I'll have some beer later on up in Campbell's room. Look, I won't be more than half an hour. I suppose you're busy. When will you be free?" Bill knew quite well that Harry wouldn't be busy, but Harry had been prepared for this.

"Well, I don't know for certain. Why don't you come up here? If I'm busy, you won't mind waiting a moment or two, will you?"

Harry hadn't seen much of him on Sunday morning. Bill had gone to have breakfast with Percy and his wife and then, after Chapel, he'd thought he ought to go and see the children in his House. Harry remembered noticing how much of Campbell's language and mannerisms still stuck to Bill, though Bill would have been furious if he'd known. And then there'd been that tiresome pre-lunch drink with Butler, a boring ritual, which it was difficult to escape, though the invitation was kindly enough meant. The difficulty was that one couldn't escape it if one went to morning Chapel. The O.Cs always went into Chapel last and they stood there, undefended victims of the Headmaster's hospitality. The drink with Butler was followed by a lunch with his old Housemaster Watson, but Bill had managed to escape by half past two. He'd dashed up to Campbell and changed out of his R.A.F. uniform into some of Campbell's old clothes and then had come up to Harry's room, where Harry had been patiently waiting, doing nothing. He heard Bill coming and had seized a book, which he was busily reading, as Bill sauntered carelessly in.

Sitting down by the stream had been enormous fun. Throwing those stones – and then those absurd races with leaves. It was extraordinary how, even when it was nothing to do really with skill at all, Bill still won. Yes, Bill's leaf had won all except one, no two, of the races down the stream and Bill had rejoiced with proud delight. Mine always got stuck on that branch sticking up across the stream; his seemed to bump it in some extraordinary way and bound off.

And then Bill had described the fun of sleeping on Cleopatra – it had been late before he had got to bed – the dullness of the drink with Butler, the pomposity of lunch with Watson, the beer being poured as though it was the finest wine, and on once again to describe, with contemptuous satisfaction, the filthy language in the R.A.F. and the idle, careless, incompetence of the officers who were in charge, men who were supposed to inspire them; but, of course, the flying instructors were different; they were O.K. And back to the thought of six months ago, to the remembered half-hours here and the hours there of supreme happiness, a happiness which could never really be evoked by the telling, a happiness which they had shared and still shared as a secret, an innocent secret, carefully preserved from intruders, and around which they had loved to weave a deliberate web of mystery.

I wonder it that'll come off next holidays. It is a bloody bore that we've got the House full of evacuees. I'm sure Mum will say we can't possibly have Bill. Bill says he is certain he can borrow that flat in London, but I know for certain I shan't be allowed up – not whilst there is the slightest chance of raids.

A siren wobbled away in the distance. Harry turned over. Is that ours? No, I don't think it is. It's funny how often when one's thinking of something it suddenly happens. We haven't had a siren for years.

Well, if ours doesn't go soon, it won't go at all. What do we do it if goes when we're out of doors? I've forgotten. Anyway it doesn't matter. Harry sat up and rubbed the sunlight out of his eyes with his clenched fists; there were little bits of grass all over his stomach. He removed them one by one. Well, anyway I've definitely made up my mind now; I'm definitely going into the R.A.F. As a matter of fact he was deceiving himself; this decision had been taken for him when Bill himself went into the R.A.F., but he liked to think he was making up his own mind. As well as this he felt a kind of responsibility; he was quite sure that Michael and John would do whatever he did. Whoever made up his mind first would in fact be making it up for all three. Strange, stray paths lead to death.

John and Michael had left Harry alone this weekend. They always did when Bill came down. The friendship between these three had matured like the whisky one reads about in advertisements. There had been no excitement: it had just developed as a result of common interests and activities. There were little interruptions. For the whole of one term Michael and Harry had seen very little of John. John had been engulfed with Dickie, but it was known only to be an interruption and not a desertion. There was no way of deserting from this friendship. Then again there'd been him and Bill. That was different of course, though I don't suppose Michael and John thought so – and now Michael was temporarily and charmingly captivated by young Robert in Campbell's House. Michael looks after him like a kind of patronising muse. When they are together they are very like an old dog and a puppy. Michael's lucky that Robert is in Campbell's House. If he was in Watson's or Rattlebones' there'd be much more difficulty, but, as it is, they can go about together whenever they want to – none of those absurd secret dates to meet behind Aunt Meredith's; none of those notes left in the hymn-book in Chapel, though in some ways the hush-hush side of it really makes the whole thing more fun. It certainly makes it more romantic. I wonder if stupid old Rattlebones realizes that his methods produce the one thing that he's trying to avoid – romance.

Harry yawned. He leant right forward and touched his toes with his fingers and then he collapsed back onto the grass. God, this is a wonderful place, this is. We will never forget it. Richard was saying that he thought boys here really got too fond of Chelborough. Someone up at Oxford told him that an old Etonian was fond of Eton in an adult way, whereas a Chelburian was fond of Chelborough in a kind of permanently adolescent way. It was an affection which never grew up. I don't really see that. I don't see how one can be too fond of a thing that's good, though God knows what sort of a place this would be without Richard and Campbell and Percy and one or two other masters. Actually it's really Richard and Campbell, I suppose.

What a lot of happiness Campbell must have had. Lucky to have been both a boy and a master here. All the happiness we've had as boys at Chelborough and then ten years teaching here. I wonder if I'll be a schoolmaster. No, I don't think I will. What a flop this place would be if Campbell got called up or anything. But perhaps it wouldn't. I suppose in two years' time he'd hardly even be missed.

Harry saw that John was sliding towards him in his peculiar way. It wasn't a walk but it certainly wasn't a shuffle. Harry waved.

"Hey-ho, Harry. Let's go down and bathe."

"I haven't got my slips with me."

"You can borrow some. Come on, you idle brute. Campbell and Co are down thee; I saw than going down."

"That was hours ago. You ran a bloody awful race, John. I watched. Wonderful scheming, brilliant planning but no results – no results. Life is not a shop window. Wasn't that a ghastly sermon? Really, I mean, a man like that shouldn't be allowed down. Some friend of Butler's, I gather. A priest from the Far East. Shouldn't be allowed. Look, I don't think I'm coming after all." Harry stopped and scratched his bottom. 'I'm sort of sulky."

John knew it was just the inevitable aftermath of Bill, but he said nothing. Harry turned and was beginning to walk away.

"No, I think I'll go back and finish that essay. If I get it done today, I can take it up to Campbell this evening and get it off my chest."

"Oh, damn you, Harry. Well, never mind. Write a good essay. It's a bloody difficult subject. I've torn mine up twice. I don't think I shall do it. Who wants to write on "Prudence?"

"I dunno. I think it's rather fun. See you this evening after tea."

Harry wandered back towards his House. He had no intention of writing his essay. He just wanted to be alone again for a bit.

CHAPTER ELEVEN

John was angry. Franklin, his Housemaster, had been very tiresome again. At least John thought so. Campbell had got one of those terrible three hour practice papers coming off on Friday and, on Tuesday night, John, having begun his essay on "Prudence" for the third time and torn it up for the third time, decided he would settle down in his room and work till all hours reading over his old essays and getting his mind in order for this three hour paper of Campbell's. He'd tell Campbell he really couldn't write both the essay and prepare properly for the three-hour paper. It was asking too much. The trouble is you could never be absolutely certain how Campbell would take that sort of thing. What seemed to you to be entirely reasonable often seemed entirely reasonable to Campbell too, but sometimes, just occasionally it didn't, and then there was hell to pay.

John hadn't been able to settle down to work till about half past ten, after having first put elaborate extra shades all over and around his light so that his Housemaster, Franklin, shouldn't see. Franklin's window was nearly opposite John's and there was no really effective way of hiding the light. Franklin hadn't gone to bed, which was nuisance: his light was still on. You could see it round the edges of his curtain, in spite of his rigid and self-satisfied black-out. What does it matter anyway? It's often happened before.

It was over an hour later that the inevitable had happened and Franklin had appeared. John had been well in the middle of reading his three essays on Luther. He loathed Luther with a hatred that was inquisitive and instinctive, rather than rational. Still, he loved reading about Luther, because it gave him so much more material with which to loathe the old hypocrite. After Franklin had gone, John had turned out his light, gone downstairs, unlocked the back door, and walked out for a short midnight stroll, and then dragged himself back up to bed. That'll mean another of those scenes with old Franklin tomorrow evening.

This time Franklin had gone a bit too far. He'd written off to John's mother. He hadn't really any right to do that. John was very fond of his mother and this obviously had nothing to do with her. She'd have a fit if she knew that he was generally up till midnight, and there would be no doubt, although she seldom supported Franklin in his many rows with John, that she would be body and soul on Franklin's side in this matter. Franklin was really using an unfair weapon. Why couldn't they just turn a blind eye to the whole thing? After all there was only another month till his scholarship, and they'd do far better to leave him alone. He must work, and they hadn't any right to stop him. That was what he was at Chelborough for and with all those Home Guard parades and farm work and A.T.C. parades, there wasn't enough time. It's all very well for Campbell to say that time is your servant and not your master, but that's nonsense. What's the good of having a servant who's always running away and never there when he's most wanted?

It was no good going to see Campbell over this, because Campbell had rather a blind spot over this matter. Campbell agreed with Franklin and was doing his best to get a kind of unspoken promise out of John that he would not stay up late more than twice a week. John had always managed to win this particular battle with Campbell, because Campbell fought the issue without any final weapon. Campbell never believed in getting to the point of asking a boy to promise anything, and John was aware of this.

Still, John had got to get all this off his chest to someone and on Thursday before tea he had dashed up to Richard's room. Fortunately Richard was alone for once. John hadn't been able to get hold of Michael. Michael and Robert had gone on bicycles to do farm work all the afternoon. Harry was no good at all at the moment. He was in a ludicrous kind of introspective huddle with himself about Bill. Tuesday had been a bad day altogether. That muddled relay and then old Franklin coming in. The interview with Franklin had taken place on Wednesday night and John was in the process of describing it to the Chaplain.

Franklin went through all the old meaningless rigmarole about me being a prefect and so, in a sense, on my honour, and then on and on about example and the fact that it was more important for a prefect to obey the school rules than anyone else. And for the entire time old Franklin was prowling around the room like a great sexless cat. Then he said that my light kept other people awake and muttered something about the blackout, and finally on to my scholarship once again, and how no one was more anxious for me to do well than he, but that if I went on like this I'd pack up. He said I was getting into a nervous state, and then, blast him, he began to quote Campbell in support. He said he'd discussed it all with Campbell and would be very glad if I'd go and have a chat with him.

"Really, Franklin is absurd," John went on, "he's always throwing out nasty little thinly disguised innuendos about Campbell and Campbell's influence, yet, he sometimes drags Campbell on his side as a kind of triumphant trump card. It makes me sick. While we were talking, Franklin stopped prowling around and started lighting his empty pipe. That always annoys me. Those smelly pipes. He's always fiddling about with them! Well, whilst he was inextricably involved, I had a brain-wave. 'Do you mind, sir,' I said, 'if I go now, I've got a lot of work to do?' And I got up. Franklin was furious, but he couldn't say anything. He just looked at me. You know that awful look, right through you, a kind of sorry, bogusly affectionate, wounded look. He just said 'Goodnight, John,' and I went out." John laughed at the memory.

"So what?"

"Well, so it is absurd, isn't it? You see, Franklin is just fussing for the sake of fussing. He doesn't really care a hoot. The whole thing is just a question of rules, rules, rules, as far as he is concerned. So long as nothing goes wrong with me whilst I'm at Chelborough, that's all he cares about. He doesn't care what happens to me afterwards. He doesn't care whether what I learn or do here is going to be any help to me after I've left. It's surprising really that one has any affection at all for Chelborough with people like Franklin about. I mean look at his sex-talks. If he really took his job seriously, he wouldn't give such ridiculous sex-talks. Well, it is ridiculous just to ignore the whole thing and treat it as though it was a dirty smell. And then one final smashing, leaving talk which apparently lasts nearly an hour and is one of the most uncomfortable things one can possibly imagine. He simply doesn't care; that's the trouble."

Richard let John go on. He was like a car that was only firing on five cylinders. Something was missing. He wasn't confident and was deliberately confusing the main issue. He was side-tracking the whole thing. Richard had noticed this sometime ago, but it was better to let John go on and get it all off his chest. Franklin was right. John was overtired; there were those tell-tale pouches under his eyes, beginning to go dark; and his eyes were almost underlined. He wasn't even attacking Franklin with his usual confidence. He's tired. I'll have to treat him firmly but carefully.

"Well, let's get back to the main point first."

There was a knock on the door and a small wispily, freckled face came halfway in.

"Sir, Mr. Campbell wants to know when you want the confirmation lists for next term."

"Oh, yes – well yesterday really. Tell him will you let me have them as soon as possible, but in any case by Saturday night. Late starters can be added afterwards."

The face withdrew.

"I don't know why Campbell always sends these urchins up. Why doesn't he use the phone?"

"Oh, well," said John, "you know quite well that Campbell has a mania about getting his boys to come up to this room in particular, and other masters' rooms in general, as often as possible. In fact I really believe his ideal would be to have all his boys scattered around in all the masters' rooms all day, absorbing pearly wisdom. You oughtn't to have sent him away, Richard – you ought to have asked him in. Anyway who is he? He looked nice."

"I forget. I did know once. The brother of someone or other who left before I came. Farquharson or Macdonald or Willams or something. I must find out. But as I was saying. To get back to the main point."

"Look, Richard, don't be too heavy. For one thing I haven't time, and for another thing I honestly don't think I could stand anyone else being heavy. And please don't quote the Angels, Richard, because they've got absolutely nothing to do with this. They've got nothing to do with Franklin."

"Actually, you're quite wrong. Still, I won't quote the Angels if you don't want me to.. Still, that's not the point. The point is that you, John, are getting overtired, or will be soon, and you ought to go to bed more often and earlier."

"Good heavens. It's a conspiracy. It's a plot. The whole world is combined against me. I am alone. Napoleon on one of those islands."

"Now, look here, John. Stop cantering round the room and listen to me for a bit."

"O.K. Richard. Let it rip. Let it rip. I know what you're going to say. Go ahead, say it, say it."

"Well, the point is simply this, or rather there are two – no – three separate points. They're more or less linked up, as most points are."

John didn't really want to hear what Richard was going to say. He'd temporarily lost interest as soon as he found that the Chaplain didn't agree with him. Still, he listened closely, once he had allowed Richard to begin.

"Stop fencing, John. First there is the simple point of going to bed. You try to confuse this with your Franklin myth and, in fact, you are being very unfair to Franklin. You told me yourself the other day that he had made what is for him a very go-ahead plan. After all two nights a week up, working late, on condition that you just nip down and tell him that you are going to stay up."

"But that's what's so absurd. One never really knows beforehand. And why should one always go and tell this old fool."

"Well, he is really responsible for you and he has the law on his side and he has suggested a good compromise which I honestly believe is in your own interest and you'd see it, if you weren't so pig-headed."

"He's only partly responsible for me. Campbell is responsible for my work and my scholarship efforts."

"Quite right. But Campbell agrees with Franklin, and so in your heart do you, John. The second point is that you don't like Franklin, and so everything becomes his fault. You feel negative towards him. You believe that you are entitled to someone like Campbell as a Housemaster, and because Franklin doesn't happen to be Campbell you vent your illogical wrath on him."

John decided not to interrupt Richard. Richard was looking a bit grim. So John said nothing though Richard wasn't right about the illogical wrath. More than that John knew what the third point was going to be. It was obviously going to be an attack on John himself.

Richard paused, took his bright red tie off and unbuttoned the top button of his check shirt. He wore a dog-collar mostly, but not on half-holiday afternoons. He got up, moved across, as he was speaking, and sat down on the derelict sofa next to John. The springs of the sofa squeaked their usual note of ineffectual protest.

"You see, John, Franklin's well over fifty, and Campbell's in his early thirties – and in many ways the balance of Franklin and Campbell is good for you. Of course I know you have an automatic distrust of anything that is good for you, but that doesn't alter the fact."

"But, Richard, it isn't a balance between Campbell and Franklin. It's a perpetual conflict. Of course they may agree here and there, over this point or that, but in general it's a conflict. Everything Campbell stands for and teaches is the exact opposite of what Franklin stands for. I can't define it in words, but you know what I mean. Campbell stands for and teaches critical thought and considered action whereas Franklin wants automatic, reflex actions, the impelling instinct being the 'Book of Chelborough: Rules and Regulations', which is given as a kind of passport to every new boy his very first weekend. God, if the wretched little boy knew what a millstone that little grey book was going to be. It's terribly badly printed, too. Not that that matters for a book like that."

"Well, you've really brought me to the third point by what you've just said, John. I think in many ways Campbell has done more for you than you'll ever be able to thank him for. Franklin's done a great deal also and is very fond of you, but I doubt if you'll ever realize that".

Richard was being very sensible; just as neutral as he was in his prayers in chapel. John couldn't help thinking of this and he remembered that awful day when Richard, in his absent-minded way had prayed for the German wounded before our own. He'd lost the thread of what Richard was saying for the moment, but he picked it up again very quickly.

"Campbell hates 'hard-thought', as he calls it, and he wants each of you to have the capacity for thinking independently and critically, in the right sense of the word. Now, in most cases this works admirably, but with some boys, I've noticed it in two or three, – Bill, for example –

in some cases this independence becomes almost a vice not a virtue. Independence instead of being a virtue becomes an affectation. And this applies to you, John, I think. You are rapidly getting to the stage when you are unable to accept an opinion either because it is the accepted opinion of a group or else because it is the voice of authority. In fact in your determination to be independent and critical, you fling away both your critical faculties and your independence. All this nonsense of not being able to work properly before ten at night and all this nonsense about rules being there to suppress individuality are just two examples of what I've been saying."

John was listening intently now. Richard could tell from the fact that he was looking away and looking down at his feet. John had kicked one of his gym-shoes off. His big toe protruded through the other.

"You see, John, if you paid a little more attention to what St Thomas thinks about individuality and personality and a little less to what Campbell thinks, you'd be a happier person. Now, in fact, you are sometimes prepared to accept traditional belief. You accept the Church and get very angry with those who don't. Just remember the times you've pranced around this room shouting 'Heretics, heretics!' about the people whose religious attitude you don't like; but the rules of Chelborough you reject out of hand, without consideration. You reject them partly because they are generally accepted and partly because they represent for you a type of authority you don't like."

John looked back at Richard. Richard really is good, you know. He felt that Richard was right. All those things that tell you, the stomach, the heart, the circulation, all these told John clearly that Richard was right. Still, he fought on bravely but without much conviction.

"But, Richard, really – you may be right in much that you've said, but you are being almost as unfair as Franklin was, when he dragged my poor, worried mother into his personal battle. It really is absurd to argue from the analogy of the Church to the 'Book of Chelborough: Rules and Regulations'. I mean if you're going to use that sort of analogy you could get yourself almost anywhere."

"No argument by analogy is watertight. Anyway, think about it, John. For the love of Michael, be different when it's right to be different, but don't just be different as kind of perpetual pose. Remember one thing, John. There have been many, many Franklins as schoolmasters in the past and their methods have without doubt produced a great many very fine men who look back at the Franklins with restrained, but genuine affection. After all there is no evidence yet that the Campbells and the Richards will do the same."

Richard leant back. "Well, let's stop all this," he said, "tell me what you've been doing, John."

"I'd love to." John put on his shoe rather languidly and moved through the door with a conscious lack of haste. He ambled down the stairs and headed back to his House.

CHAPTER TWELVE

Peter Campbell has asked Richard to take prayers in his House on that Friday evening. In other Houses evening prayers were compulsory but Campbell has decided that House prayers, which took place on Mondays, Wednesdays and Fridays, should be voluntary in his House. Oddly enough there had been little comment on this among the senior Housemasters. It was the sort of thing you would expect Campbell to do. One or two of them had subsequently thought about it, but had rejected it for two main reasons. First, Campbell did it, and that was a strong reason for not doing it. Secondly it was very convenient to have the whole House assembled once or twice a week so that one could give out notices, congratulations and communal rebukes. Campbell apparently didn't feel the necessity for this. His prefects gave out any necessary public announcements and he seemed to find that casual meetings with the boys and his perpetual contact with the prefects made any official mass rebukes very rarely necessary. In any case to have House prayers as an excuse for House notices hardly seemed justifiable.

Campbell viewed House prayers rather seriously. For one thing he would only allow the Head of House to read the lesson. This guaranteed a certain continuity and also avoided the sensational novice. If Campbell knew that some other prefect really wanted very much to read the lesson he used to arrange for the Head of House to be absent from prayers on school business, but on the whole either Campbell or the Head of House read the lesson. Most Housemasters had a short lesson, the Lord's Prayer, one other prayer and a blessing, but not Campbell. The lesson was never less than fifteen verses and as well as the Lord's Prayer, Campbell always read three or four other prayers.

It was odd really. Campbell standing in the middle of the passage, with a bright light over his head so that he could read, but not bright enough to see the boys who lined both walls, facing inwards towards him on either flank. The Head of the House stood opposite him and the other prefects were grouped at either end. Campbell always said that prayers were only compulsory for him and the Head of House, but in fact the boys liked the friendliness and the atmosphere and never less than about eighty percent attended. After all one never knew. Perhaps the Chaplain might come; he sometimes did, and when he took prayers it was marvellous.

Richard had come up to Campbell's about two minutes before prayers were due to begin, apparently completely unprepared and a little breathless. The prefects were waiting and as they went through, to the House passage, Dickie shouted: "Come out to Prayers, now." Doors opened, and slippered, dressing-gowned figures filed out. The shuffle ceased and Dickie began to read, not very well. It was the parable of the sower and it seemed to go on for rather long. The light wasn't very good. We'll have to get a better bulb, thought Campbell.

Richard said the Lord's Prayer quietly, and then he prayed for the House. It wasn't so much an extempore prayer as an adapted prayer. He looked up as he prayed for the boys, their parents, their brothers and sisters, the old boys of the House, and the servants. Richard paused after each to give the boys time to whisper a name or two to themselves. And then Richard looked back down onto the floor and prayed for the Headmaster and the Masters and for the School Mission in Bethnal Green, and lastly for God's blessing on the Chapel. Somehow the fact that he never used a book, but just prayed appealed to the boys. Campbell never took his eyes off the Chaplain, throughout. The boys realized that Campbell had the greatest admiration for Richard.

And at last Richard looked up again and gave the blessing. He called on Christ and the Virgin Mary and the blessed Angels to watch over and guard the boys and he made the Sign of the Cross. There was a slight pause and then Campbell led Richard out, back to his room and poured him out a glass of beer.

"Don't be too long drinking this Richard. You must go back into my House."

"But I can't Peter, I can't! I've got boys coming up to see me tonight."

"Well, you must put them off that's all."

"But I can't do that. I can't possibly."

"Well, you've just got to, that's all there is to it."

"Oh, all right then. I'll just go in for ten minutes."

Peter Campbell went in with Richard, and found a small boy and sent him off to Richard's room to tell the boys that the Chaplain wouldn't be there. He knew quite well that once Richard was in the House, he wouldn't leave for at least an hour. Having done this, Campbell went back to his room. He had tried to keep this Friday clear as he wanted to begin correcting the three-hour history papers.

He was halfway through the first one, Hugh's, when there was a shuffle of slippers outside and a knock at the door.

"Come in."

Campbell looked up after a moment and Roger was standing there. Roger, who was in Campbell's House, was a good-looking, athletic boy, of the-out-door, dog-and-horse-loving type. The coat of his best holiday suit had two slits up the back. He was a simple but extremely pleasant boy. His father was an Indian Cavalry Officer. His mother was dead. He had no really close friends, but everyone liked Roger. About a week before Campbell had told him that he was going to be a prefect next term. Roger was in his pyjamas and dressing-gown but he hadn't washed yet, or else he hadn't washed very well. There was a large dusty smudge across his forehead just under his rusty hair.

"Well, Roger, what can I do for you?"

"Are you, busy, Campbell?"

On the whole only the prefects called Peter Campbell by his surname, but apparently Roger did too.

"Well, yes and no."

"I would rather like to see you, if you are not too busy, sir. I tried last night without success and tomorrow night I'm on Home Guard duty."

"Oh, that's quite O.K. Sit down. You prefer the armchair to Cleopatra don't you?"

Roger sat in the armchair and Campbell leant against the mantelpiece. In an absent-minded way he had a cigarette alight in each hand.

"Well, Roger, what's on your mind?"

"Paul."

"Which Paul? Paul Grant or Paul Stocker?' Both were in Campbell's House.

"Paul Grant."

"Tell me about it, Roger."

Paul Grant was a boy of about fifteen, a good athlete with a sparkle in both eyes, lively but not particularly good-looking.

"Well, sir, it's never happened to me before."

"What's never happened before? Have you stolen something of Paul's, or what?"

"Good heavens, no, sir."

Campbell knew quite well that he hadn't, but when a boy seemed to find it difficult to get something off his chest from a home-fire sense of guilt, Campbell always shot some question to the boy which could be confidently and vehemently denied and repudiated. This gave the boy both relief and confidence. Campbell knew quite well that Roger's growing affection had settled on Paul for the moment. He had noticed it about a fortnight ago and was waiting for Roger or Paul to come through to see him. He hoped it would be Roger. He had decided to give them a fortnight and then, if neither had appeared, to get hold of Roger.

"Well, sir, it's like this." Roger hadn't quite got used to calling Peter Campbell by his surname yet.

"Look here, Roger, would you like me to talk for a moment or two and then you can go on from where I leave off."

"Yes, Campbell, that would be marvellous."

"O.K, then. But stop me if I go wrong or you want to say anything. You will, won't you?"

"Yes, I will. I promise I will." Roger leant back into the armchair with a good deal of relief. Now it no longer seemed to matter that the cushion wasn't quite right and was humping into his back.

"Well, about three weeks ago whilst you were bowling to the smalls at a net, or whilst you were taking them in their last practices for the gymnasium competition, or perhaps was while fooling about in the swimming pool, you suddenly found that it was fun to do things with Paul and that he seemed to respond in a different way from the other smalls to what you were saying. He seemed quicker and more anxious to learn and, though he didn't say anything, you felt he was grateful. He was a bit dumb in some ways, but you didn't mind that. He used to seem to say a lot with his eyes and that odd little shrug of the shoulders. It's really more of a flick than a shrug. Am I right so far, Roger?"

"Yes, yes – more or less. No, actually you're plumb right. It was at the nets. Dickie couldn't get down one day, nor could Alex or Reggie, and I was asked if I'd go down and take it."

There was a pause. Roger apparently wasn't yet prepared to go on.

"Well, shall I go on for a bit?"

"Yes, sir; go on for a bit."

"You didn't take a great deal of notice of it at first. But without any conscious planning, you used to find some reason for speaking to Paul if you bumped into him in the passage, and he seemed pleased, and from time to time you went along to his room to borrow a book, which you didn't really need. And so, without your really noticing it, you gradually began to think about him whenever your mind wasn't fully occupied, and you used to watch him in Chapel, even if you could only see the back of his head two rows away in front of you. You had begun to resent his other young friends who had so many normal opportunities of meeting him and being with him. In fact you began to disapprove of them, to imagine that Paul would really rather be with you if he had the choice. When you were out of the House, you began to wonder from time to time what he was doing and you even began to plan your day, as far as possible, so that you would bump casually into him from time to time. You looked up the time-table to see which classroom he would be going to for a certain lesson and then you would try to walk round that way, rather slowly, so that you would have more chance of meeting him. And you used to curse the Master who let him out late. Probably you were tricked altogether one day when he was at music instead of being in School. If he wasn't in Chapel you were panic-stricken in case he was ill and in the Sanatorium

It was difficult to define really what it was. You just wanted to be with him or if not that, to see him and get a responsive smile. You feel you've got something to give him which his younger friends, Jim and Robert, haven't got. You're quite glad that Robert sees such a lot of Michael in way. It takes Robert away from Paul. And, when I told you a fortnight ago that you were going to be a prefect you were terribly pleased, and, though I asked you to keep it to yourself for a bit, you had a tremendous desire to tell Paul. He could be trusted. You began to plan in your own mind whether or not you could get him as your room-fag next term. He was Dickie's this term, but Dickie was leaving. Would Alex or Reggie want him? That was the point."

"Yes, but then I remembered he'd be in the Middle First next term and wouldn't be a fag at all."

"That was a bit disappointing, wasn't it?"

"Yes, it let me down with the hell of a bump."

Another pause. Campbell didn't believe in long pauses.

"Well, how right am I?"

"Practically entirely. Little bits are wrong. I mean, for instance, I didn't tell him I was going to be a prefect."

"Well, actually Roger, I didn't say you did. I just said you wanted to tell him more than anyone else and you felt he could be trusted completely.

"That's true enough. And I didn't feel I'd be good for Paul. I couldn't be good for him; he's much better than I am."

Campbell remembered that he hadn't said that either, but it would be childish to contradict merely to score a technical point.

"But you do feel you've got something to give him? You do feel you could keep an eye on him don't you? You don't altogether approve of his friends, do you now, Roger?"

"Yes, I do; no I don't. I mean I do think I can help him a bit and I don't altogether approve of his friends. But how did you know all about this, Sir?"

"Well, first I am not entirely blind. Secondly I can remember my own schooldays fairly well, and boys run far truer to form than horses or dogs; but perhaps I can explain it best to you like this." Campbell got up. He never sat still for long. He was about to light a cigarette when he noticed that he had already got one.

"Well, it's like this." Campbell paused again. "Just over two years ago, one summer term – it was the summer term of 1941 – on an evening very like this. Yes, it was after House prayers, I can remember it quite well. I'd been playing cricket that day and was in white flannels. A boy came in, just a shade older than you are, Roger, and he said 'Campbell, can I see you for a moment?' and he sat there, or rather over there on Cleopatra, and he told me all about a very nice boy called Roger and, bit by bit, piece by piece, he told me most of the things about Roger that I've told you about Paul. It's odd really, isn't it?"

Roger momentarily went a little white. He leant forward in the chair as he spoke.

"God, yes. I think I know who you mean. If it was Harold, he was really very nice but I never thought twice about him. He was just rather fun and I was sort of proud of knowing him and being seen with him occasionally. It gave me a kind of position, I suppose. Of course it also meant I got hold of little bits of School and House news when they were still official secrets. He asked me to go and stay with him in the holidays."

"But you didn't go, did you? I was rather sorry you said 'No'. It was I who suggested to him that you should go."

"Good God. Did you?"

There was another short pause. Roger felt much better. It really was extraordinary.

"Did Harold disapprove of my friends?"

"Yes, yes. He was very strong on that. Thought you were with a bad unhealthy set. Wondered what he could do about it."

"How ludicrous! It was only Alan and Peter. How absurd!" This is really is ludicrous. Surely Campbell can't be making the whole thing up. No, he couldn't be. He wouldn't make up a thing like this. "What did you say to Harold as he sat on Cleopatra?"

"Well, I told him that he was growing up and this was just one of the normal signs. I asked him if he'd ever lost his heart in the least bit to a girl and he said that he hadn't. Have you, Roger?"

'No, not really. In fact, not at all."

"Then I told him that this fluttering heart for Roger – it was fluttering for you, you know –this fluttering heart and this imagining all sorts of unlikely incidents in which Harold and Roger were the chief actors, all this merely meant that he was just ready to fall in love with a girl."

"But, I don't think I ever shall. I meet so few."

"Well, you will very soon. Once you leave here at the end of next term you'll meet lots. You ought really to be meeting them now, but it isn't awfully easy to arrange at Chelborough. In the meanwhile don't worry about it. Just keep a sense of balance. Remember what you thought about Harold. Remember that whatever Paul may say with his eyes, the chances are that he really far prefers his own casual friends, whom he hardly even realizes are there at the moment. And there's one last question, Roger, are you really fond of Paul?"

Campbell had come over and was sitting on the arm of Roger's chair. Roger looked up at him.

"Yes, Campbell, there's no good pretending I'm not. I'm very fond of Paul. You know that, don't you?"

"Yes, I thought you were. It's not a question of pretending. It's just a matter of speaking your heart. But it you are really fond of Paul, and there's no reason why you shouldn't be, after all he is most awfully nice – just a shade grubby at times, but that's all right – after all he's only fifteen." If you really are fond of him, and I know you are, that makes it easier for me to ask you to do one or two things for him. First, let him choose his own friends. Choosing friends is one of the things you've got to learn by experience, however bitter the experience may be. However strong the temptation, don't try to interfere with this. Secondly make sure not to let Paul remember your friendship for the fact that it allowed him to know the newest news before his contemporaries. It's too easy a bait to catch a young fish with. Lastly do nothing that is going to lower him in his own eyes or those around him. You know their standards and how jealous they can be. Do nothing to spoil the immediate life that is his, a life which, although you are only two years away from it, you cannot enter again. The gates are closed. Apart from that, do all that you and Paul want to do, both of you. Do anything and everything as long as it doesn't lift him out of his environment too suddenly and, above all, make sure that neither of you have no regrets. If you're in doubt, just say to yourself, 'Will I ever regret this?' and more important, 'Will Paul?' And don't boast about your friendship to other people; at the same time don't let it be a secret, don't be ashamed of it. Talk about it, but don't boast about it. Some of these things obviously don't apply to all friendships, but most of them, I think, do. Try to see to it that your affection for Paul and Paul's affection for you is a really happy one."

Peter Campbell moved off the arm of Roger's chair and went over and sat on Cleopatra. You couldn't really sit on her. It was more lying than sitting.

"I hope I haven't been too heavy, Roger, but I really mean what I say."

Roger said nothing, but he looked happy.

"Fetch the biscuits, Roger. I managed to get some chocolate ones. They're in the cupboard outside."

Roger was glad to go outside for a moment. He was very happy, but also just a little sad. He came back and put the green tin box on the floor. It had the image of a Scotch terrier on the lid. Its tongue was hanging out.

"Would you like some lemon squash? Do have some. I'm going to have some beer."

Richard came in, as usual without knocking. He had been much longer than he had meant to be in visiting Campbell's House.

"Did you enjoy yourself, Richard? You know Roger, don't you?"

"Yes, – Roger? Roger? Yes, of course, and it's high time you came and had tea with me again. Why don't you bicycle over with me to the 'Canterbury' on Sunday for lunch? Two or three others are coming. You know – Monty, Basil, Michael and Robert and somebody else."

"I'd love to. Will that be all right, Campbell?"

"Of course it will."

"Why don't you bring someone with you, Roger?" Richard beamed down at Roger.

"Oh, I dunno. Perhaps I will. Can I let you know tomorrow?"

"Yes. But don't trouble to let me know. Oh yes, you'd better; one more or less. One has to let the people know nowadays how many are coming. Especially after that trouble we had last time with the goldfish pond."

By the time Richard had told the terrible and reprehensible story of the goldfish pond at the "Canterbury" and Roger had countered it with a holiday story of the bar at the Coliseum and another story, a very involved one about a duster and a drawing pin and an older temporary master, most of the chocolate biscuits had vanished. But Richard hadn't yet told the full tale of his trip round Campbell's House.

"Peter, you can rest content. You've got a grand lot of boys."

"You're right there,' said Roger, "you're plumb right."

"Richard and Roger left together, Richard to go back to his deserted

He took the receiver off. "Can I have 299?" The operator, a girl said "Yes, but would you like to take an incoming call first?"

It was Watson. "I've got bad news."

"Yes," said Campbell. "I've got young Harry up here. He told me. I was just about to ring you up."

"Bill's mother rang up during lunch. No details, I'm afraid, but there is no doubt about it. None at all. It's a bad show. I am sorry for his father. Well, will you forgive me? I must ring the Chaplain and the Headmaster. Butler will be very upset, I'm afraid."

"Thanks awfully," Campbell said. It seemed a silly thing to say.

He walked over to Harry, who was still very white, and put a hand on each of his shoulders.

"Yes, Harry, it is true." Campbell had once had to tell a boy that his father had been killed, but it had been far easier than this. "There are no details yet, Harry."

"I don't want any details. I never want to know any details. Details don't matter." And Harry looked up at Campbell as though to say, 'You never knew Bill as I did,' but the words never came.

Campbell looked away, still with a hand on each of Harry's shoulders.

"I knew Bill," he said, "but not in the way you did. And I am terribly sad, so I know, Harry, what you must feel. There's nothing I can say that will do any good – no good at all."

Harry leant forward and put his head on Campbell's shoulder. He was a shade taller than Campbell, and he cried. It was a feeble kind of crying, not weeping, but it seemed to help Harry a bit. Campbell dropped his hands on to Harry's arms and held him there for a few moments; then he led him over to Cleopatra and plumped him down.

Harry looked up. He began to mop rather feebly with his handkerchief. "Sorry. Campbell," he said, "But that's much better."

It wasn't really. It only helped for a minute to two.

"Why don't you go up and see Richard later on? He'd love to see you."

"I don't want to see Richard. I hate Richard. I hate Michael. I hate John. I hate you, Campbell. Richard would only tell me that it is selfish to be sad. He'd say that Bill is happier now and that our friendship isn't broken but strengthened. But that's a lie. It's a lie, Campbell. It's true that not even death can take the past away from us, but it has certainly taken away the future. Death is all right for martyrs and saints – I remember reading that somewhere – but Bill isn't a saint or a martyr. He's just Bill. Bill isn't meant for death."

It's odd how he still uses the present tense, thought Campbell.

"Look, Harry, I've got to go. We each really want to be alone. Would you like to stay up here? You can lock the door on the inside and I'll put up that silly little notice, – 'Do not disturb' – on the outside of the door. I'll be gone for well over an hour and you can stay or go, just as you like."

"I'd like that. I just can't see anyone at the moment."

"Well. I'll just go next door and change into my old flannels for this miserable farm work, and then I'll fix up the notice."

Campbell was back in a moment or two

"You know where everything is, books and photos and things. Just lock the door from the inside, and I'll shout when I come back, if the door is still locked. Don't let anyone else in."

And Campbell went off down the stairs. He walked down to the farm. He didn't feel like bicycling. In any case he had heaps of time. Alex and Reggie were coming up the path. The news had obviously got around. Campbell gave them a tired, slightly self-pitying smile.

Campbell's sadness had been partly swallowed up in Harry's. He was more concerned just at the moment with his sorrow for Harry than with his own personal sorrow for Bill. That would be awful when it came. But at the moment the thought of Harry made him feel a little faint and slightly sick. He remembered Watson telling him that in the last war people got used to this kind of thing very quickly, but he couldn't believe it. You couldn't get used to this. It wasn't possible. But subsequent events proved to Campbell that Watson was right. Campbell began to think of people other than Bill, young Chelburians whom he couldn't bear to die. It made Campbell feel better. The realisation that so many were still alive was a comfort. He was in fact deliberately keeping his mind off Bill. He wasn't ready yet to think about Bill, but it was impossible completely to keep his mind off Harry.

As the path hit the main road Campbell bumped into some of the smalls from his House. They were going down to the farm too. There was a cluster of five, and among them were Paul and Robert.

"Hello, Robert, I thought you did farm work all Thursday and missed tea into the bargain." Campbell couldn't help thinking of Michael whenever he talked to Robert.

"Sir, is it true that Bill Revery's been killed?" Paul was speaking.

"Yes, I think it is."

"I remember him so well my first rugger term. He was marvellous. Do you remember that match against Rugby, sir? He just ran through them; they couldn't touch him. He was terribly good, wasn't he, sir?"

"Yes, – he was very, very, good."

"Do you think he'd have been an international?"

"Well, you can never tell, Paul, but I think so."

"It's terrible sad, isn't it, sir?"

But it wasn't terribly sad for these boys. To them Bill was part of their conversation, a remote figure on a rugger field in dark blue and light blue, or teaching some lucky small boys the simpler points of hockey on a bumpy ground. For them Bill was an incident, a phantom figure.

For Campbell, Bill was one of the few Chelburians who had seen through him. Campbell had always looked forward to Bill's visits, even though he scarcely saw him at all when he was down. He hadn't been at all jealous of Bill's triumphs. That's what it was about Bill; no one at Chelborough was jealous of Bill. Everyone, small and old, master and boy, seemed to regard his triumphs as their own. That wasn't true of all boys. Campbell left the farm a bit early. He told the boys he was sorry to let them down by going early, but he'd got some work to do, and he walked rather quickly back to his House.

Harry had not really quite known what to do when Campbell had gone. He had picked up an Auden, but Auden hadn't got anything to say. Nothing at all. Surely Wilfred Owen must have something. I remember a poem about "red lips"; but Harry couldn't find it. He glanced through "Dulce et Decorum est". No, it was no good. It was meaningless. He picked up Campbell's photo album. There were masses of photos of Bill there, mostly in teams and harvest camps. There was one I like very much. Where is it? Damn – I know it's a loose one. Here it is. It was one of Bill after a game of rugger. It had been taken by some press man, and there was Bill, absolutely unruffled, standing sideways, in his light blue and dark blue striped rugger jersey. It had a wasp-like look in the photograph. He had his hands on his hips and one stocking was round his ankle; he was obviously being charmingly polite and modest to someone else, who wasn't in the photo. Campbell had cut the photo down, rather raggedly, so that only Bill was in it. I must ask Campbell who Bill was talking to. I'll take this photo and tell Campbell afterwards; he won't mind. He doesn't really value it. Anyway it isn't really fair that Campbell should have all the photos of Bill, whilst I've only got two – and one of them is terrible.

Harry spent some time looking through the album, but he stopped when he reached the generation before Bill. He left the album open on Cleopatra and walled over to the history papers still lying on the floor. His paper was on top, the next to be corrected. Campbell will dash through my paper as quickly as he can and then get me up here and go through it with me. He'll want to get me back to normal as quickly as possible. I wonder when people will begin to try to cheer me up. Campbell will try. He'll put everything on the material level.. Anyway I don't want my bloody scholarship now. There's no point in getting one now. There's no one to tell if I do. I really only wanted one because Bill got one. Richard will be different, but Richard won't be any good. He'll just make me more miserable, and he'll be miserable too. John and Michael will be the best. They just won't try, but even they will make a rather obvious effort to be natural.

Harry went over and lay on Cleopatra. His mind wandered back over the lovely and obvious things – Bill's visit last weekend; he took out Bill's last letter and read it through. One page was crumpled. He'd crumpled it up by mistake, thinking it was something else. Harry smoothed it out again. Harry was beginning to feel lonely. He was glad when he heard slow footsteps, deliberately languid footsteps, a knock and a shout – "Harry?"

Harry unlocked the door.

"I've bagged that photo, Campbell – the one of Bill with his stocking down. You don't mind?"

Campbell did mind. It was his favourite photo of Bill.

"Look, Harry, make some tea. I'm going to change. Go and make some tea, whilst I wash my grubby paws and change my clothes."

After changing Peter Campbell slipped over on his bicycle to the married Housemaster, Percy, who still had a car and a little petrol.

"Percy, can I borrow your car? Young Harry won't start talking properly about Bill. I've got to get him talking freely. He is still using the present tense. I want to loosen him up. Can you lend me the car to take him over to the 'Canterbury' for a couple of drinks? I can't take a boy down to the local 'Old Maid of Perth'. I'm afraid it'll take about half a gallon and I can't repay it."

"Certainly do. Peter. I'm terribly sorry about Bill. Harry. I imagine, is very upset. He'll get over it in a week or two."

"As a matter of fact, Percy, I don't agree with you. I think it will take him quite a year, possibly two. He's going into the R.A.F. Perhaps he won't live long enough ever to get over it."

"Oh, I don't know. Anyway, good luck. Here's the ignition key and the back tyre's not very reliable. There's a good spare, though. The tools are under the driving seat."

After tea Campbell suggested to Harry that they should drive over to the "Canterbury" for a drink.

"I've borrowed Percy's car."

"Really, Campbell, occasionally you do manage to do quite sensible things."

On the way to the "Canterbury" very little was said. It wasn't until the third gin and lime that Harry really began to open up. The saloon bar was deserted; it was a bit early yet. Harry was sitting on a stool and Campbell was leaning against the bar. There was a stupid looking stuffed owl in a glass case over the empty fireplace. Both Campbell and Harry were smoking cigarettes.

Harry said. "I remember the irritating way in which Bill always insisted on listening somehow to the nine o'clock news wherever he was and when people protested, just looked round perkily saying 'There's a war on.' And the bar billiards. That table at the 'Crown" that had a slope to square leg. If you got three or four balls down that side you could go on for ever.

"I always thought you and Bill were rather selfish over that table. You always had some inviolable reason why you simply must have one more game."

"Bill got rather drunk one evening."

"Yes, and so did Dickie. It didn't matter so much about Bill, but he ought never to have let Dickie get drunk. Dickie was far too young then, – or now for that matter. So was Bill really."

"Still, Bill learnt his lesson. He was awfully nice a bit drunk, wasn't he?"

And they chattered on – Campbell thought three gins was quite enough. On the way home in the car Harry turned to Campbell and said, "Do you know, this is the first time I've ever really felt the war."

"Yes, it's funny the way it's suddenly burst in on us with a bump."

"It hasn't any right to really, Campbell. You see the rest didn't count. It's different, of course, but one got used to it. I mean going down to the shelters, and farm work and the Home Guard and no hot water or ices. All those were nothing more really than dropping Latin and taking up German".

"Yes, I suppose that's right."

"Do you know, Campbell, the miserable thing is that I shan't have any sort of goodbye from Bill. He won't have written since he came down to Chelborough and that other letter was just saying that he was coming. Last weekend he said that before he started operational flights he was going to do up a lot of things in an enormous envelope, poems and letters and odds and ends, and address them to me, – just in case anything happened. But this was only a practice flight. He won't have done that, will he?"

"No, I'm afraid he won't. Still, didn't he write in that book? He said he was going to."

"Yes, it was silly really. He just wrote a line out of that song. He said he couldn't think of anything else. He just wrote: 'I'll be seeing you always.' It seems absurd now, doesn't it?"

As they drove into the School drive Harry just put his hand on Campbell's arm very gently and said: "Thanks awfully, Campbell."

"Oh, it's nothing. I enjoyed it. It did me good."

Peter Campbell saw no more of Harry that day. Later that day Richard came up.

"Peter, I've just realized that tomorrow's lesson is David and Jonathan."

"Well, that doesn't matter, does it? It's not a bad thing really – at least so long as someone decent is reading it."

"Yes" that's all right. It's Franklin. He reads well. But the point is I was going to preach on it. Ought I to revise my original intentions and take Bill into account or shall I not preach on it at all or shall I just preach as I originally intended?"

"If you preach on David and Jonathan, at least a third of the boys will be thinking of Bill, and some of Harry – and many of the masters, too; if you preach on that, you must take Bill into account. It would be cowardly not to. After all, what's the church for, of it isn't prepared to deal with what is in people's hearts?"

"I'm not sure. Fond though I am of Bill, I'm not sure that one should always consider the immediate."

"Well, I don't ask a favour of you often, Richard – but now just one. To please Harry and me, preach on David and Jonathan. It won't do me any good, but if you're in any sort of form it'll do Harry a lot of good. In the pub tonight he told me that he was never going to marry now. I'm sure nothing you say to him in private will do the least good, so you might as well have a crack in public."

"Yes, I think I will. Somebody's bound to be furious."

"They probably will be, but what does it matter. One gets used to that."

"Well, in that case I must dash off and readjust my thoughts. I think you're right, Peter. Sorry for the interruption – Goodnight."

Campbell was pleased. Richard was bound to be good. He always was on this sort of occasion. It was something to look forward to.

CHAPTER FOURTEEN

Herriot was sitting in his fellow Housemaster Watson's room after supper. Watson had rung him up to ask him to come over for a chat, and obviously he was in the process of going around his House. The door leading out to the boys' part was ajar. He shouldn't be long now. I'll just take one of his cigarettes and wait. Herriot went over to the silver cigarette case on the little round bogus 18th century table. He looked at the lid; on it was engraved "D.B.W. from C.F., J.V. F., R.F., and P.L.F. in gratitude." Four brothers I presume who were in his House long ago. I imagine by the time I've been a Housemaster as long as Watson I shall have a lot of engraved silver trinkets. I imagine there is more of the parent than the boy behind most of them. Boys' minds don't move along the recognised adult lines of gratitude. Watson, he knew, was a bit of a games player in his day. He's getting on now, but he keeps remarkably fit really; never seems to get tired. I suppose it's because he thinks so little. Herriot thought of that description of the regular officer who was so stupid that even his fellow officers noticed it.

However, in spite of the fact that Watson thought upon simple lines and was a good fifteen years older than Herriot, Herriot had a great respect for Watson's instincts as a schoolmaster. Watson gained a good deal of strength for his opinions from Herriot's obvious admiration, but most of the strength came from his conviction of his own rightness. Herriot began to think of Harry and Michael. Really as prefects they had given him far less trouble than he'd expected, but still no one could call them good. They weren't in the House often enough. Still, they were keen and obviously much attached to it. They had a good way with the younger boys, too. Yes, I was right to make them prefects in spite of the risk involved. They would have been an impossible nuisance if I hadn't.

Herriot heard a door slam. That must be Watson, he thought. Herriot knew quite well why Watson has rung him up. It was to discuss this afternoon's Housemasters' meeting. Every third Thursday this particular body met at the Headmaster's House. It was a nuisance as it rather spoiled the half-holiday; not that anyone really got a half-holiday nowadays, but one liked to cling to the illusion of a free afternoon. The meeting had been troubled, though very little had been said. It was getting near the end of the term and the thorny topic of House plays was first on the agenda. Second was the question of lights-out, and third was the question of tips to the stewards by leaving boys. All the trouble had occurred over the first question. The atmosphere was so strained after this that very little discussion took place over items two and three. In fact it had been one of the shortest meetings on record. Campbell had been very childishly tiresome.

Watson come in.

"Sorry to have kept you waiting. Would you like a whisky?"

"No, later, I think, if I may."

Watson, after assuring Herriot how glad he was he had been able to come up, and generally beating about the bush for five minutes, eventually came to the point. Watson does waste a lot of time, thought Herriot.

"What did you think of that Housemaster's meeting this afternoon, Herriot? To be quite frank, I don't think it reflected much credit on Chelborough. I wish now that I had said more at the time. It isn't that one doesn't think of things to say at the moment, it is just that one is nonplussed by the attitude of some of those who have rather less experience than they have voice." Watson chuckled noiselessly. That was rather a good epigram.

"Yes. I don't think Butler was firm enough. He was resolute at the beginning, but when Campbell made that yattering speech, he really should have told him to shut up or something."

"The trouble really is, Herriot, that Butler pays far too much attention to what Campbell and the Chaplain say. I remember quite well, earlier this term, when he asked me up to his House to give him my opinion on a certain matter, I spoke my mind and all Butler said was: 'You must remember Campbell has been here man and boy for sixteen years' – well, that may be true, but I've been a master here for over twenty – and, damn it. I taught Campbell myself. I remember him quite well – rather grubby he was as a small boy, though I must say he was always more than useful at games. Never really fulfilled his promise, you know – lacked guts, though I don't like to say it. One always gets the impression with him, in spite of everything that he's not really out of the top drawer."

"Butler was quite right. It all worked all right, Watson, before Campbell and one or two others allowed their boys to choose their own plays and censor them themselves. Of course there were very few House plays in the old days and it was easier, but House plays are infectious things and infectious things are unhealthy. If only all the Housemasters would have the guts to censor their own plays, it would be all right. After all we are here to try to teach the boys some sense of morality. It is simply begging the question to assume, before you start, that they have already got it."

"I agree with you, Herriot; I must say, I agree with you. And if some Housemasters adopt this attitude, then Butler was quite right to lay it down in black and white that he had decided to establish a central censoring committee composed of masters. I, myself, can't see why there should be any objection. The people he named are good, broadminded, young, but sensible chaps."

"Personally I thought Campbell's remark was impertinent and, as so often, not entirely to the point. It was unfortunate, but typical, that the Chaplain supported him."

"It's unfortunate I think that the Chaplain so often supports the younger Housemasters in their refusal to shoulder their traditional responsibilities. Take this matter of preparation for confirmation. It's all part of the same thing. I can't see why a Housemaster should shirk the very onerous and fatiguing duty of preparing his boys for confirmation. Of course the Chaplain should have some say in the matter, but primarily it's the responsibility of the Housemaster. After all many of us have had what almost amounts to a lifelong training in it. I find that confirmation preparation, above all, does give one a very real chance to get to know the boy. You have him by himself. I myself regard it not only as preparation for confirmation, but also as preparation for the other sides of life, if I may put it like that. Of course, one wouldn't mind the Chaplain playing his part, if only it was honestly possible to agree with much of what he said."

Herriot felt that, even allowing for Watson's experience, this was becoming rather a one-sided conversation. He offered Watson a cigarette, but Watson didn't seem to notice and went straight on.

"The Chaplain doesn't even insist on the boys whom he prepares learning their catechism. I must say that if Campbell's and Percy's parents knew the whole in-and-outs of the thing, I can't believe they would agree with having their boys prepared for confirmation exclusively by the Chaplain. If you don't mind my interfering in what is none of my business I can't believe that the Chaplain's influence has been altogether healthy as far as those two historians of yours are concerned. It's difficult to say anything about Campbell's influence because he is after all their official mentor." Watson liked that word. He decided to use it again. "And after all, I suppose the official mentor must be allowed some say."

"I agree with you. As a matter of fact I'd already decided to go and see Butler about it. I think the Chaplain has done a good deal to upset young Harry over your Revery's unfortunate death, but still that's a small thing, and I've no doubt he tried. I do feel however that he might have taken me into his confidence. The Chaplain's influence on both Michael and Harry has I think been mainly bad. He will treat them as adults. It's absurd and pretentious. They are little more than children. It's just as bad to encourage a boy to grow up too quickly as it is to discourage him from growing up at all."

"I'm glad to hear you say that, Herriot. It coincides almost exactly with my view of my boy, Hugh. Really the way these boys develop one begins to doubt if one is really wise in letting any boy at Chelborough do history. Of course they do get scholarships, but it is at a very great price. I can't believe that Campbell or the Chaplain has done Hugh any good at all. He sees far too much of the Chaplain and I frankly believe the Chaplain is largely responsible for Hugh's precocious attitude, I have written to his father, and earlier I had to write to young Brittain's father on much the same lines."

"Well I'm going to see Butler about my two. The trouble is, Watson, that Butler is too broadminded. He isn't really capable of taking a firm decision."

"Well, I'm going to see him too. I'm going to see him again about Hugh and also about one or two other similar things. I'm also going to see him about the preparation for confirmation, – I know Butler doesn't agree with the Chaplain's views on this – and, to be absolutely frank, I'm also going to say that I honestly don't believe that the Chaplain understands what co-operation means. I'll admit he comes to me from time to time to discuss a boy, and is often quite helpful, but far more often he is perverse and independent.'

"I would go further than you, Watson. I would say, whether the Chaplain intends to or not, that what he says to the boys actually has the effect of setting the boy against his Housemaster. I must say that I have found Harry and Michael far less co-operative in the last year since that have got to know the Chaplain really well. Campbell has somewhat the same effect, too."

"Yes, that goes for my Hugh, too. What is worse, though, is that this attitude is beginning to spread among the younger boys. They seem to be losing all sense of values."

Watson leant forward and felt his forehead. "I suppose I should be called old-fashioned if I were to say that they are losing their sense of loyalty." He leant back again.

"And since we are being quite frank," said Herriot, "and I agree with you that it is better to be quite frank over these things, I think there's a good deal too much drink about, both in Campbell's room and the Chaplain's. Now, I don't for a moment pay any real attention to the stories that some people spread around to the effect that Campbell is constantly giving his boys drink, but he's much too free and easy in the way that he has beer about the room. I don't think it's healthy for boys to see their Housemaster drinking beer on and off throughout the evening. I remember going up to Campbell's room to see him one Saturday evening. There were several O.C.s down for the weekend – not, of course, the better type of O.C. – and there were several boys there and, of course, Campbell. There's no other word for it, the whole room smelt like, well, like a beer parlour. The Chaplain's not quite the same thing, but he is always taking boys off on their bicycles on Sundays to the 'Canterbury' and one can never be sure what goes on there. The difficulty is that one can't very well refuse permission to a boy to go off on a Sunday with a master, and yet one's quite certain that the parents wouldn't approve.

That's the trouble. One's first duty here is towards the parents. I mean we would be very awkwardly placed supposing something happened at the 'Canterbury' and a parent then said to me, 'Did you know that the Chaplain gave them drinks?' It would be very, very awkward. Take the other day for instance, the day young Bill Revery was killed. It was a Sunday I think."

"No, – two Saturdays ago."

"Well, that doesn't really matter; but I am pretty certain that young Harry – you know him – I'm pretty certain he spent all the afternoon and most of the evening with the Chaplain. I didn't like to ask him anything. He was obviously a bit upset – rather unnecessarily upset, but I've told you about that already. Well, when he came up to my room his breath smelt very distinctly of gin. I thought of saying something to the Chaplain about it, but what's the good? Of course it doesn't matter so much for Harry – after all his father drinks like a fish – but it sets such a bad example in the House."

"Yes, it's time someone took a much firmer line. It's time someone really spoke to the Headmaster. Why don't you, Herriot? I've spoken to him so often. I don't like to say it, but I don' really think that he pays very much attention to what I say."

The clock on the mantelpiece gave one thin, bored note.

"It's quarter past ten. Will you forgive me if just go up and see that my prefects have put their lights out. I've had a lot of trouble with them lately. Some Housemasters don't seem to care what their prefects do. Then, of course, one's own prefects naturally get to hear of it and think one is being unreasonable when one insists on their keeping the rules. It's getting a harder task now, day by day, to do one's duty."

Whilst Watson was away Herriot looked round the room. He knew it so well. Watson's desk, – at which he spent so many hours, and yet it looked as though no one ever went near it; just a blotter, a long round black ruler, a revolving silver calendar, an inkpot, a rubber stamp, a penholder and the mark-book on the far corner. One photo stood by the inkpot. It was a brown faded man. Herriot wasn't sure who it was, but he believed that it was Watson's old Housemaster at Sherborne. Round the walls were signed photos of successful House teams. I wonder if my House will ever be capable of being cock at anything. One pretends not to mind, but it would be very nice for a change. On top of the bookcase, huddled together, were photos of Watson's old boys, each in a silver frame. A great deal of time was spent in polishing the unfashionable furniture, though from a material point of view, it was scarcely worth the effort. On the sideboard was a small silver cup. Herriot had often examined it before. It was a cup for High Jumping that Watson had won in 1907 at Sherborne.

CHAPTER FIFTEEN

"It's put one in a very awkward position." Campbell was up in in Richard's room. A parallel discussion to Watson's and Herriot's was going on there. "You see, our House was already in rehearsal and of course I'd already told the children that the full responsibility for censorship was theirs. I pointed out to them what I thought were the one or two errors of taste which were made last time and, on the whole, I think they agreed. Old Rattlebones at Friday's Headmaster's meeting said that giving the boys the responsibility was just shirking one's own, but that's absurd. Of course a Housemaster is finally responsible for whatever goes wrong in his House. It's just a question of how he uses that responsibility. Rattlebones really made me angry."

"As a matter of fact," said Richard, 'the one thing Rattlebones and Co are afraid of is responsibility. People who are afraid of things going wrong shouldn't really be allowed responsibility. They just lean back on the book of rules like a smug cushion."

"Well, after this pronouncement by Butler I was awkwardly placed. One's got to accept it until we can get it changed. But it was no good my sending for Alex and the rest of them and saying that it has been decided to set up a central censoring body and that I'd changed my mind and I thought that was a very good idea and would they be ready to take all the scripts along."

"What did you do, Peter?"

"Well, I thought a lot and then I sent for Alex and one or two of the others and I told them this central censorship had been set up. Then I told half a lie. I said that in some ways it was not a bad idea, but went on to stress to them that as far as I was concerned they weren't to shirk their responsibilities. They must censor it first before they submitted it to the official censors. I said I should be very angry if the censors had to make any real changes after it had been submitted to them. They asked me if I'd like to see the scripts after they had done the preliminary censorship and I said: 'No; it was entirely their own concern.' Was that fair on the whole, do you think, Richard? It isn't sabotage as far as I can see; it certainly isn't meant to be. In this way I have left the boys with a kind of diluted responsibility which is really the best I can do. The trouble was that Butler didn't submit the whole thing to a discussion, he just announced it as a decision."

"Yes, and I was bloody angry. I wanted to make the point that these kinds of things are far easier to impose than they ever are to remove. These temporary regulations have a way of becoming accepted permanencies. His answer was absurd. I mean it's absurd to say that the censorship would be kept on until the boys had shown themselves capable of decent public taste. If everything is to be officially censored, how is anyone ever going to decide when that time as arrived? As a matter of fact my own view is that this will just act as a kind of challenge to the boys – another thing to get round. They'll try out everything on the expectation that the censors will miss something, and, of course the censors will. Then one can't hold the boys or the Housemaster responsible. No wonder those old buffers were so delighted with the idea. It removes all final responsibility from their shoulders on to an outside body. If those chosen four had any guts, they'd refuse to serve on the censoring body, but, of course, they won't."

"Yes, I mean, take a simple example – there are always bound to be four or five funny and improper jokes circulating round the school at anyone moment which few, if any of the masters would know. It would be perfectly easy for the boys to write or adapt a sketch, take one line out of each joke and put it into the script. It would get through the censors every time, and when the night came, there would be roars of pornographic laughter from all over the hall. Boys are ingenious animals and there are masses of things like that which they could do, and, what's more, I'm quite sure that if you take all responsibility away from them most of them will. They'll consider it no longer a matter of their own taste and quite divorced from any question of morality. In that case Butler will be in a perpetual state of righteous horror, and I suppose the end will be that the boys, having shown themselves incapable of censoring and the censoring board having shown themselves incapable of censoring, there will be no House plays at all, until the boys have shown themselves to have sufficient private taste to be capable of submitting scripts to the public censors.

"Yes. 'Here we go round the prickly pear'. It's a farce, Richard. I don't see how the boys are ever going to acquire what Butler calls 'public taste' unless they are given some opportunity. Of course, if you leave it to the boys, giving them always a certain amount of retrospective guidance, there will be mistakes made but I guarantee there will be far more under this scheme and, what is more, they will be worse in a way. They'll be deliberately schemed and plotted mistakes. I don't see how the boys are ever going to learn anything, unless you give them the opportunity of making mistakes. After all, it's far better they should make them here where the results are not so devastating and where they have some sympathetic guidance. Anyway, I'm going up to see Butler about the whole thing tomorrow, Of course he won't change his mind. He seldom makes a decision but, when he does, it's like one of those great clumsy heavy rocklike things. You can't move it. Still, there's no harm in trying. One's never any worse off for a 'No'. But I was right, Richard. It wouldn't have been any good pretending to those boys that I'd had a sudden revelation and all that I'd ever said before about the importance of them being fully responsible for their own productions and my refusing even to see the scripts was suddenly all baloney, and that now a new dawn had appeared and the perfect solution had been devised. They'd have seen straight through the whole thing at once."

PART III

TAKE IT OR LEAVE IT

CHAPTER SIXTEEN

It was after lunch. For several days Juliet had been worried about her husband. She realized, of course, that towards the end of a long summer term the Headmaster was certain to get tired. He didn't seem really to want her to talk to him. Instead of sitting with her for about half an hour after supper as he generally did, he had on each of the last few evenings mentioned the great amount of work that he still had to do and had gone off after a few minutes to his study. On two occasions he had left his cup of black coffee only half drunk. Obviously he had something on his mind. His voice was tired. Once at supper Juliet had plucked up her courage and asked if he was worried. All that Butler had said was: "No, darling, no more than usual," and so she had let the matter drop. Life would be much easier for him, she thought, if only he had a child. A child about the House would take his mind off the school. Well, thank goodness the roses are good this year.

Butler had been very worried for the last few days. He had reached his decision last Monday, three days ago. Twice he had gone to the telephone to ring the Chaplain up and both times he had turned away. He must think it over again. He must be quite certain that he was right.

Butler was sitting this Thursday afternoon in his study up at his house. He had asked the Chaplain to come up to see him there because he particularly did not want to be disturbed and Richard was due in about half an hour. It was impossible to settle down to do anything else, and Butler began to think over, once again, why he had decided to tell the Chaplain that he must leave Chelborough at the end of this term. On one thing he was quite decided; if the Chaplain was to leave, he must leave straight away. He wasn't the kind of person you could have around for a whole term under notice to go. Still, that was a minor point. The decision to tell him to leave had been a far more difficult matter.

First, Butler had to quite certain in his mind that he wasn't giving way to the line of least resistance, Without the Chaplain it is true there will be no more of those never-ending interviews with men like Watson and Franklin. Even Herriot, who is a very calm dispassionate man, was up last week to complain. Four Housemasters in one week was a lot. All the complaints were different in kind, but similar in principle; they all amounted to lack of confidence in the Chaplain's influence on the boys and what these Housemasters considered to be non-co-operation on his part. None of them had accused Richard of deliberate non-co-operation; they had implied that it was inherent in his nature. Each of them, except for Herriot, had also referred to Campbell, but they seemed to look upon him as a minor problem. He affected far fewer of their boys and their chief objection to him was obviously the manner in which he ran his House, and to a lesser extent the History sixth; still, that was really no concern of theirs. The question of the Chaplain was different.

My trouble is that I have too many things on my hands. The Chaplain and Campbell really only have to worry over the boys. I wish they were my only worry; in that case I should see far more of them than I do. It is quite true that probably Richard has his finger on the pulse of the school to a greater extent that anyone else. I am quite sure in my mind that when in difficulty, many more boys go to Richard than anyone else, I wish, in many ways that more of them would come to me. Yes, I must be careful to be quite certain that jealousy is not behind all this in my case. To some extent it is in the case of Franklin and Watson, but I am quite certain that is isn't so in mine.

And the other trouble is that I like Richard. One can't help liking him. He may do foolish and occasionally do irresponsible things, but he is so openly honest. Fresh, I suppose, is the word that best describes him. There is no doubt at all that some of the life will go from the school if Richard goes. As against that, however, it is true that the four senior Housemasters all feel that his presence and influence undermine their work. Richard, of course, has the full support of Campbell and a certain amount of support from Percy and from one or two of the younger masters, but many of the other masters don't seem to think a great deal of him. It is true that most of them are oldish men and temporary masters. They haven't any real interest in the School when it comes down to it. I myself feel that to some extent Richard undermines even my own authority. I think some of the boys resent the fact that I am not wholeheartedly behind him, but, much as I admire a great deal of what he does, I can't really support him to the full.

It seems as though my talk with him at the beginning of term about co-operation with the older Housemasters hasn't had very much effect in practice. If anything, the whole thing has got rather worse. What Richard won't seem to realize is that in a great institution such as this you've simply got to be capable of subordinating your own opinion from time to time to the opinion of others. Richard doesn't seem able to do that. There's something inside him that won't let him. He lacks the virtue of compromise. That's what it is. It was shown quite clearly over this censorship trouble last week. He wasn't even prepared to accept my decision. Such a situation really becomes impossible. Campbell was nearly as bad over that. In some ways he seems to get more truculent every day.

What'll be the effect be on Campbell? Of course he'll be very upset, but I think he'll soon forget. He's so bound up in the boys in his House, the historians and the rugger, that he'll forget as soon as next term is started. I shall have to be prepared to see him about it, of course; he certainly won't take it lying down, not if I know anything about Peter Campbell.

And the boys? I can't be certain about that. Roy Hodgson, the Head of School, doesn't really like the Chaplain, at lease from what he said to me the over the weekend I don't think he does, and he implied that there were plenty of others who didn't rally approve of him either. I rather believe his influence on the boys is slightly exaggerated by Campbell. After all, Roy ought to know. It's a pity I haven't time to be more in touch with the boys. It is comparatively easy for men like the Chaplain and Peter Campbell, but I have to busy myself with so many other things – the staff, the timetable, the buildings, the governors, the grounds, next term's new boys, preparatory school headmasters and goodness knows what else.

Butler got up from his chair and went to look out of the window. It was a stormy sky and he turned away. It isn't the Chapel. I know it isn't the Chapel. I don't approve of everything he does but I do honestly believe that his work, once he is inside that building is first rate. It'll be difficult to find another man anything remotely as good; still, it's too big a price to pay. The point really always gets back to the same thing. So long as Richard is here most of the older masters will be thwarted or at least feel thwarted. There'll be perpetual bickering and jealousy. The decision isn't really hard to make. I can't conceivably get rid of the others. In any case, even if I could, I'd still decide against Richard. All that has held me back so far this last year has been the real hope that he would become more reasonable. No, I never imagined it would be as forlorn a hope as it has proved to be. It's an ugly decision to take and it may mean a certain amount of unpopularity, but I don't see that I really have any choice.

The sound of a bicycle swinging up the short circular drive, a squeak of ineffective brakes and a muttered "damn", plainly audible through the open window, told Butler that the difficult moment had come. He went over to his desk as if to write a letter.

Richard had felt that this was going to be a tiresome interview, but he had not been prepared for this. When Butler began by telling him of his decision, Richard went very white and, for a moment, he stopped thinking altogether. He didn't really listen very closely to what Butler said after that. His mind kept wandering back to the cricket ground, and to Michael, John and Harry. He thought of the Chapel and the Harvest Camp which he was going to run at the beginning of the summer holidays. His mind didn't settle anywhere. It jumped backwards and forwards. He heard occasional words and sentences of Butler's. "Franklin   reasonable   Chapel."

Butler was surprised that Richard accepted the decision without any argument. "What about the Harvest Camp?" was all that Richard said.

"I was coming to that. It's at the beginning of the holidays and it's a work of national importance and I'd like you to carry on with it, if you feel you can. It would be very difficult to replace you at this stage."

"Oh, I'm glad. I'd like to. That's good." Richard was still a little white. He looked a little whiter than he really was. It was partly the effect of the bright red shirt the he was wearing. As so often it was open at the collar.

"One other thing, Richard. I feel this news is going to upset a lot of people. I personally intend to say nothing about it to the masters till after the boys have gone. I imagine you'll want to tell Peter Campbell, but I'd rather you told no one else. Ask Peter to keep it to himself. I don't want to deprive you of the chance of saying goodbye to your friends among the boys, but I think most of them will be with you at your Harvest Camp, won't they? I feel it would be better if you said goodbye to them there and told them the news then. What do you think?"

"I think that's right – quite right."

"Well, Richard, I don't want to keep you on a half holiday afternoon. This hasn't been easy for me, as you know."

"No, I know. Well. I'll be going. I don't quite know what to say." And Richard went. Butler was staggered that the interview had been so short. He'd put aside two hours for it.

Richard bicycled away rather slowly down the big gravel drive, up to the main buildings. He propped his old bicycle against the gate of the Chapel and went inside.

CHAPTER SEVENTEEN

Friday was to be extra half-holiday in honour of the V.C. which had just been won by an old Chelburian and the first round of House matches was going to be played. At Chelborough there were eight Houses. This was very convenient as it made it easy and comfortable to have a quick knock-out competition. Campbell's House was reasonably confident of winning the cricket Cup. They had what was, on paper, certainly the best team. They had been drawn against Watson's House in the first round and it was likely to be their toughest match. Campbell's House had beaten Watson's very easily and were about to dispose of Rattlebones' with even greater ease. It was a cold July afternoon. There were great heavy bruises across the sky, but so far there had been no rain. The weather had been fine and hot recently, and this sudden cold day got underneath one's mood. One wasn't really ready for it after the warm spell.

Campbell was sitting on one of the three wooden benches under the copper beech tree, on the same bench as the two scorers. On the other two benches sat the batsmen in Rattlebones' House. Rattlebones was sitting in a deck chair, swaddled in an overcoat and looking terribly cold; in another armchair sat his wife. As Campbell looked over at them he thought how odd it was that schoolmasters' wives always seem to have either about ten children or none at all.

Rattlebones' House was not doing very well, though perhaps a little better than Campbell had expected. No one was making many, mostly fives and tens, though one agricultural batsman had made thirty. Four or five wickets were down. Campbell wasn't quite sure which. He got up and moved over to the scorers – oh, five.

It wasn't very exciting. Surely Dickie's going to take himself off. No, he's taking his sweater off again. Campbell's mind wandered away to Harry. He had seen very little of Harry since the evening of Bill's death. It seems as though he is deliberately avoiding me. I asked John, but he said Harry had said nothing about it. That was a surprisingly good shot. Yes, of course, Dickie would move the fieldsmen now! Fat lot of good it was blocking the last shot instead of thinking of the next one. It seemed really as though Harry had begun to regret letting me in on his private grief. I can't see how he can possibly get a scholarship now. My idea of taking him right off history and putting him on to sixteenth and seventeenth century art and the moderns certainly hasn't worked. It's done no good at all. It's all having a rather depressing effect on John, too. Good heavens, I was wrong. Another wicket. Same shot again, but lofted this time. Extraordinary what dividends the idiocy of boys sometimes produces. Yes, John needed the stimulus of friendly mental co-operation with Harry. Hugh doesn't really provide that. I hope Harry's diminishing keenness won't unduly depress John. I must get Michael on to John. Perhaps, if Michael started working a bit, John would too.

They must be nearly a hundred. Campbell walked over again – 96 for six. Well, anyway, thank goodness Dickie's taken David off and given Reggie a bowl –about time too. Reggie had less technical ability than David and Dickie but he had the advantage of bowling much straighter. He took the last four wickets very quickly. All out for one hundred and seven; it probably wouldn't have been much more than seventy if Reggie had been given a bowl a bit earlier. Still it doesn't really matter; I can't see how they could ever get us out for under two or three hundred. It was a single innings match.

Dickie walked over to Campbell, obviously rather pleased with himself.

"Cunning change of field that! Did you see it, Campbell? That man looked rather like getting set."

"Well, I don't know how cunning it was, but it was certainly effective. Look here, Dickie, if you and David bat for as long as you bowled I'll have no complaints."

"O.K. Campbell, You just watch," and Dickie went off and put his pads on.

I'd better go over and say a few words to the Rattlebones duet. Campbell walked over. He shivered a bit as he went. It certainly was damned cold. Rattlebones was just getting up as Campbell reached him, and his wife was folding up the tartan rug which had been trying to keep her warm.

"Hello, are you off? I thought young Smythe and Rawlins batted bravely and well."

"Yes, I thought they did well. We got more than I thought we would. Not nearly enough, though, I'm afraid. It'll be another massacre, and I don't feel like staying to watch it. I think I've done my duty for a cold day like this, and I've got a tremendous number of reports to write. Have you done yours?"

"Oh, yes. I've got most of mine done, I must admit."

Campbell far preferred it when his own team was batting. He was always a shade nervous for the first over or two, but it was fun sitting with the children and listening to their cricketing profundities. On this occasion there was no particular reason to be nervous. Dickie and Reggie got away to a very quick start and thirty was on the board in no time.

"Looks as though I shall be able to take my pads off very soon." Alan was speaking.

"Touch wood. Touch wood."

"I don't suppose I shall get an innings again today."

"Well, personally, I rather hope you don't, Paul; if we're still behind them when you waddle in as number ten, I for one shall be a bit depressed." Campbell leant forward and grinned confidently at Paul Stocker.

"Anyway, thank goodness it'll all be over fairly quickly and we shall be able to get away for the early bathe."

There'd been a change of bowling and Dickie pushed the first ball away off his pads just in front of the square leg umpire for a longish looking single.

"Yes," Dickie called and dashed down the pitch as though he intended to get two.

"No," called David. Dickie managed to stop and turn about halfway down the pitch.

"All right. Come on," David shouted, and began to run.

A simple return to the bowler and the bails were gently removed. In the confusion it was difficult to be certain which of them was out. Dickie walked back looking rather sheepish with a shamefaced grin.

"Apparently David thought the square leg umpire was a fielder. It was my call, wasn't it?"

"Yes, I think it was."

At Chelborough the umpires in House matches were not neutral. Unemployed batsmen from the batting side umpired and their decisions were erratic. Sometimes this was the result of an over scrupulous sense of fairness, sometimes just from ignorance. On this occasion miserable little Paul Grant was umpiring at square leg without wearing a blazer. He certainly did look like fieldsman.

"I should take him out a blazer at once. It'll cheer David up and imply that it isn't general considered to be his fault. It doesn't matter depressing Paul."

Reggie had played the rest of that over confidently and scored a couple. The first ball from the new bowler to David was quick and very short. David moved across to hook it and missed. It hit him on the waist.

"How's that?" First slip appealed in a rather vague way. Up went Paul's finger without hesitation. David couldn't help looking surprised. It was such a very surprising decision.

"Paul isn't doing too badly as an umpire" Alex said. "At first sight one couldn't be certain which side he's on."

David was a bit cross when he came in, but not very. It didn't really matter very much. Thirty-four for two was quite good enough. Eighty for six wickets wasn't so good though. Reggie was still there but had begun to bat with exaggerated care and his partner was following suit.

"If they go on batting in this way we shall need another twenty-eight byes to win. I think it's optimistic to imagine that that will happen." Campbell tried to keep cheerful, but it was all very exasperating. He looked across to the right and saw Butler wheeling his bicycle across the grass. Lord, he thought, I hope he isn't going to stay long at a moment like this. It's no time for polite conversation. Butler leant his bicycle against the copper beech and came and looked over the scorers.

"How's it going, Campbell?"

"Not too well, I'm afraid. I can't pretend the bowling is very good. They are just getting themselves out. Another twenty-five to get and four wickets to go."

"You ought to be all right. Wish I could have got down here sooner, but I'm afraid I couldn't. As a matter of fact I know Headmasters are supposed to be neutral in House matches, but I shouldn't be at all sorry to see them win. You've had lots of successes recently and it would cheer them up. They're not a bad side are they?"

"Oh, I don't know. Not bad really, I suppose. As a matter of fact we are all a little biased in this corner. We hope the best side wins, so long as it's us."

"Well, I must get along down to the other game. Have you heard how it's going?"

"No, not a word."

Butler went back and picked up his bicycle. He wheeled it off towards Aunt Meredith's.

"Not exactly a bundle of tact, is he, Campbell?" Dickie was speaking. "I'm going out to umpire next, and it'll have to be a very straight ball to get me to say 'out'."

Reggie was next out, caught at the wicket, and another wicket fell soon afterwards. Paul Stocker got up to go in.

"Well. it's happened, sir. Are you depressed?"

Campbell was a little taken back. He hadn't time to answer. It was all over ten minutes later. Ninety-six was a miserable score. They hadn't the heart to go down to Aunt Meredith's, they just walked dejectedly back to the House.

"Well, you are a lot or rabbits." Campbell spoke with bogus cheerfulness.

"I wouldn't have minded so much if the game itself had been fun, but it wasn't."

My dear David. That's absurd. If we'd happened to make twelve more runs you'd have thought it one of the most amusing and exciting games you'd ever had. If you're going to measure your enjoyment of the game by the result, you're an even bigger bunch of miseries than I thought. After all, in spite of what everyone says, it is only a game, and if you can't enjoy a game you'd far better not play."

"Dear, dear," said David. "You're obviously out of sorts, Campbell."

"Yes, I am. Of course, I'm just as disappointed as all of us, but it makes me angry when other of you say that you didn't enjoy what really was an exciting and amusing game."

"But you weren't out l.b.w. to a ball that was going for four byes. I can't imagine how Paul can possibly have thought it was dropping on to the wicket."

The first drop of rain fell, but no one took very much notice. Campbell turned up his coat collar.

"Well, we'll have to see that we do better in the rugger next term and I'll have to organize some 'punt-abouts' to practice enjoying losing."

"Thank goodness I shan't be here for that," said Dickie with an infectious laugh. "I can't imagine anything more depressing."

The rain began to come down really hard; it was almost hail and bounced viciously off the tarmac path. There was a moment's indecision and then Campbell led a mad rush towards the House. They weren't very far away, but by the time they reached it, Campbell was a bad last and had begun to walk. He was a very bedraggled figure as he shook himself in the doorway.

CHAPTER EIGHTEEN

Campbell was lying in bed. He'd been lying there like this for some time. It was long, long, after midnight but, for once, he was fast awake. He didn't really want to go to sleep. It seemed an unfair thing to do on a night like this. Poor Richard, I wonder if he's awake.

Richard had come up to see Campbell about eleven that night. I shall never forget Richard's face as he told me the news. All the life seemed to have gone out of it. Dead it was, really. He couldn't seem to remember quite what Butler had said. All he seemed to remember was Butler saying "inherent non-co-operation". – I can imagine him saying it – and constantly talking about Watson and Franklin. God, it's a triumph for those two, and I bet you old Herrriot and Rattlebones had something to do with this. I wonder if they know yet. Oh, no; Butler said he wasn't going to tell anyone till after the boys had gone. It won't be easy keeping it to oneself, though it will be much harder for Richard.

It would have been better if Butler had agreed that I should come up and see him tonight. After all, midnight isn't all that late. Waiting till tomorrow night will be an awful strain. It'll give me time to change my mind too, which is a pity. I can see John still, looking up at me the other day and saying, "What would you do, Campbell, if for any reason Richard was sacked?" It was a strange question. I never really meant the answer seriously, because the whole thing seemed so unlikely. Still, it's just as true now as it was then. If Chelborough has no use for Richard, then it hasn't any use for me. I don't want to go. I've always imagined myself here, forever. In spite of all of them, I've been wonderfully happy here; too happy probably, Richard would say. And Richard, too; of course, he would have gone soon after the war anyway. However happy he was, he'd think it wrong to stay in a soft job like this, but I'd never thought of going. Never. Leaving the children would be terribly difficult, but perhaps it won't come to that. Perhaps something will happen, though I don't know quite what. I doubt if I shall be able to convince old Butler;

he's not the man to change his mind. Richard didn't seem to know if he's consulted any of the governors about the whole thing. That's the crucial point; if he has and they've agreed, then there is very little hope. He'll never go back in it in that case. I wish Richard had paid more attention to what Butler said; that's typical Richard though; he never seems to listen to things that only concern himself.

I couldn't get him to see that this didn't really only concern himself. If only he had, he might have put up some kind of a fight; now I shall have to fight all alone, and I'm not at all sure how good I am at that. I must ask Richard if I can consult Percy, but he's sure to say that I can't. God, if I go on like this I'll never get to sleep. I'll damned well get up. It's the only thing to do. I'll go into the sitting-room for a bit and have a cigarette. Peter Campbell got up, and shuffled into his slippers and put on his dressing gown. He walked over to the window and looked out. It wasn't raining now. You could see moonlight through the gaps in the running clouds, but there didn't seem to be a moon anywhere about.

I must have a cigarette. Damn, they're in my coat. One never goes to the right pocket first. If I find them in the first pocket it will mean that everything's going to be all right. Now, which am I most likely to have put them in, left or right? No, that's cheating; I must just try my luck. I should probably have put them in the right-hand pocket, so I'll make it as hard as possible. I'll go to the left-hand pocket first. Campbell ferreted his hand into the left-hand pocket; he felt under the handkerchief. Yes, they were there. He took one out, fumbled on the dressing-table for some matches, and lit it.

Peter Campbell cycled down to Butler's house. He looked down at his trousers. It would have been better really if I had put on a pair of grey flannels. I meant to. These blue corduroys had more than had their day. I know Butler hates them. Still, I had no time really.

Butler had gone out of the room to fetch Campbell some beer. He himself was evidently going to have a whisky and soda tonight.

So he had told the Governors, at least the only two effective ones, and they've agreed with his decision. Things don't look very good. And he expected that I would come up to see him to fight the battle. My telephone call didn't surprise him. The only thing that surprised him was that I didn't ring up earlier. Well, we haven't really got down to it yet and I shall feel more confident with a glass of beer. I mustn't be distracted by the mincing way in which Butler sips his whisky, not unlike a woman smoking an unaccustomed cigarette. His lips never seem to touch the glass. I ought really to be thinking about what I'm going to say; still, I've thought it over so often, there isn't really much point. If one plans these kinds of interviews too carefully it simply doesn't work. One can't rely on the other person saying the things which he should. Then if he doesn't, one's put off. I've probably thought about it and planned it too much already.

The door was pushed open by Butler's tray. A glass wobbled and slipped down the tray towards him. He edged round the door uncomfortably.

"I'm sorry about all this, but it's the maid's evening off. I don't know what we'd do without Lucy. My wife's always terrified she's going to get married or something."

"Oh, I shouldn't worry, Headmaster. She doesn't appear the marrying sort. It would require a brave man to marry Lucy."

"I'm not so sure. I think only a really timid man could face it." Butler almost smiled as he spoke. "Still, let's get back to the business if the night. Oh, would you mind putting your glass on the table? I never trust beer on the floor. It has a way of getting kicked over."

Campbell, slightly irked, picked his glass up and put it on the table. The table was on his left hand side, which was annoying. He hated drinking left handed and it meant he would have to tie himself into a knot every time he wanted a drink. He pushed his chair back and swiveled it round a bit towards the table.

Butler had already begun to rub his knee.

"I think, Campbell, it would be better if I said a little first. It will save both of us time, I think."

"Yes, do."

"Well, I said just now, and I don't think that it is in dispute, that this is in no way a personal matter. I am actively attached to Richard and will miss him very much. You will, too, I know. However, I am convinced that there is nothing worse for boys than to be presented with an open conflict between those responsible for their discipline. There is no reason at all why Richard should approve of Watson's or Franklin's or anyone else's methods or of what I may call the more formal, traditional approach. There is no reason why he should even use them himself. There must obviously be room for plenty of variety of method. A static society at a school like this would be disastrous."

"Yes, but…"

"No, don't interrupt me yet, Peter. Let me go on for a bit."

Butler was rubbing both knees now.

"Unfortunately, Richard is unable to conceal from the boys his complete disapproval of the methods of Franklin and Watson. The result is that the boys become confused. Authority is brought into disrepute. Good advice is rejected because it comes from a mouth that has been ridiculed. I must say, Peter, that you, too, are not immune from criticism in this respect. I have tried desperately hard to get Richard to see and accept this. I have assured him that I realize that as Chaplain I do not expect him to use the methods of others, but I do expect him to respect them. At last I have become sadly convinced that Richard is either physically or morally incapable of this. I am determined at this vital stage in the life of the boys that they shall not be bewildered and confused. They have a right to expect to have here a staff which is fundamentally united and which is capable of presenting a united front over most matters. I have come to the conclusion that so long as Richard is here that such a united front is an impossibility. That being so, Richard must go. I had no alternative, Peter – no alternative at all. No one could have tried harder than I have to make Richard see reason. I don't believe that there are many people sorrier than I am to see him go."

There was a pause. Butler leant forward and picked up his glass. He tipped it under the soda-water syphon and there was an empty gurgle. Campbell picked up his glass of beer, took a sip and put it down on the floor.

"May I say a word now, Headmaster?"

"Yes, Peter – of course."

"Well I think there is a very great deal in what you say, but the thing is not as one-sided as you think. The point is that Richard and Percy and I don't come bumbling up to see you and complain every time that Watson or Franklin or old Rattlebones – sorry – abuse us in public. I can assure you that they have often said things to the boys about Richard and myself which it would be fair to say implied a complete lack of confidence in our capacity for looking after boys. These have not been isolated cases. Just to quote one. A boy told me, and I have no reason to doubt him, that Watson was talking to him over some problem, and the interview came to an end. As the boy got up to leave, Watson said: 'I don't want you to go off now and see the Chaplain to pour out all your troubles to him. It's a waste of time. You might just as well pour them down the drain.' Now, I believe that Watson did in fact say this, and there have been plenty of sarcastic, destructive remarks about me as well. But the difference is this. Richard and I don't really mind about those kind of remarks. We are not afraid of them. Richard, I am sure, believes that what he stands for and says is not injured by those kinds of attacks. On the other hand Watson & Co are nervous and sensitive, and they are nervous because I believe that in their hearts they know that they are wrong, but they are too old to change their methods, just as I perhaps shall be too old one day to change mine. I can promise you, Headmaster, that Richard has given more public support to those people than they have ever given to him."

Campbell suddenly noticed that Butler was looking at his glass of beer on the floor. It certainly was very near his foot. Campbell picked up the glass, took a gulp and put it back on the table.

"What is more I don't necessarily agree with you about presenting a united disciplinary front. You wouldn't suggest that the boys should be presented with an exclusively Tory interpretation of history any more than they should be presented with an exclusively Marxian one. You wouldn't suggest that boys should only be allowed to read 'good' books or see only 'good' films. You would expect to give them some choice, some experience so that they are capable of forming a standard of judgement for themselves. Well, these boys are mostly going to be officers or to hold jobs in which they themselves will have to exercise discipline. It seems to me that we have an obligation to make it clear to them that discipline isn't a standard product, that it can't be mass-produced, that it is open to variation. Above all I believe it is our essential job to make it clear that any disciplinary system, which is not founded on consent, is morally wrong. Discipline must be a partnership between boys and masters. It cannot be of value to the boys if it is something imposed upon them."

"They're too young, Peter, They're too young. This isn't a University. That is the mistake that you and Richard always make. You treat the very young as though they were adolescents and the adolescents as though they were grown-up."

"Well, that may be a better fault than treating the adolescents as though they were very young. The trouble is that authoritarian discipline is so easy, so much less trouble to those in authority."

"I can't help it, Peter. I'm sorry that you can't agree with me. I didn't think you would."

"But look at it from another angle, Headmaster. I am now going to speak my mind, and I believe that you will agree with much that I say." Peter Campbell shuffled in his chair. He wanted to get up and walk about but he resisted the temptation. Peter leaned back again. A clock in the hall outside started striking the hour. It must be ten o'clock.

"Richard's the hell of a man. Any boy who has got into any kind of close personal contact with him – and there are a great number of them – swears by him, as do the young masters. I have no doubt in my mind that he is the best master here, and when I say that I am not excluding present company from my mind. He devotes his whole day to the school and most of the night. When he's not caring for the boys, he is caring for the servants, and I may say that he is about the only person who does. Compared with him the rest of us are all idlers. There will be a great number of boys who will never forgive you or Watson or Franklin for this. They will consider that you have done the school a mortal harm. Then there are the recent generations of old Chelburians to consider. They won't be in very much doubt. After a year or two Richard will be forgotten here, but he won't be forgotten elsewhere. There are too many young Chelburians who love Richard for that to happen. Many will remember you, in the years to come. They will tell stories about you and will hold you in a certain amount of friendly affection, but Richard will not be in their minds, he'll be in their hearts. They associate Richard with Chelborough. When they think of the school and plan to come back and visit it, their minds turn first of all to Richard. You're cutting off a leg and leaving behind a cripple."

"Yes, Campbell, but sometimes one has to cut off a leg to preserve the body."

"But this isn't necessary. It isn't necessary. If there were more of the younger masters here, you wouldn't think Richard's methods so exceptional. You have never seen the school as it normally is. At the moment the younger masters are away at the war. It's top heavy. The school is top heavy with age. You think that the Watsons are normal and the younger masters are abnormal. You're wrong. All that's happened is that this war has given the older men a devil-sent opportunity to rear their ugly head, and you are helping them to do it. If you allow them to impose upon you, it will take ten to fifteen years to undo the harm that they will have done to Chelborough. I'm sorry. I'm sorry. Perhaps I've been too outspoken. Still, it can't be wrong to speak what's in your mind."

"Yes, so long as it is your mind and not your heart that's speaking, Peter. You seem to have forgotten, though, that I have consulted people who knew Chelborough well, people who knew it before the war. I consulted them before I reached this decision."

"People who pretend to know Chelborough well may not really know it as well as they pretend to. I don't think there is a single governor who knows Richard properly or in any way intimately. I don't suppose any of them has even met a Chelburian who left in the last four years and who talked seriously about the school. Absentee landlords were almost a blessing compared with our pretentious governors."

"That's hardly relevant, Peter."

"It is relevant, Headmaster. It is. What is more, if I may say so, you are succumbing to the greatest temptation which the Devil places before intelligent planners. You are, of course, consciously and deliberately planning this school. That is a right thing to do. But it is always easier to plan for uniformity than it is for diversity. To plan for diversity requires supreme patience, and you are in the process of yielding to the temptation of planning for uniformity. In any association which has culture as one of its chief objects that is a tragedy. It's almost better not to plan at all."

"Well, I can't see that we are really getting very much further, Peter."

"Does that mean that there is no chance whatever of your reconsidering your decision?"

"None, Peter. None at all. It is not a decision that I have reached lightly or without thought."

Peter Campbell got up and began to walk about the room. Butler watched him.

"Well then, I must say my last word. If Richard goes, I go too. If Richard isn't good enough for Chelborough, than nor am I. I agree with all that he stands for; the only trouble is that I am often too idle to do all that I should. I should feel a traitor to remain here. I couldn't do it. I shall leave at the end of the term. I can't have it said that Richard was too good for Chelborough, but Campbell wasn't. I've made up my mind. Richard won't want me to leave, but I shall go. Perhaps I ought to have gone and joined up long ago."

"You've thought about this, Peter. This will make a lot of difference." Butler paused. "You're leaving your own boys and your historians behind. They can't go with you. You're deserting a lot of people, many of whom have come to rely on you. Of course, if you have really made up your mind, I can't ask you to change it. I can't pretend that it's altogether a surprise, but I had hoped it wouldn't come to this. Think it over, Peter, and give me a ring or come and see me in a day or two."

It was a very sad Campbell who walked home to his House that evening. It was very dark, but he tried to see the familiar landmarks. Only a week to go. Perhaps this may be the last time that I walk down this road.

CHAPTER NINETEEN

The last day of the summer term at Chelborough was traditionally a Monday. The boys went home very early on the Tuesday morning. Some pretense was made of going to school on the Monday morning, but most of the masters either read to the boys or allowed them to read to themselves. In the afternoon you could go to Old School and buy your ticket for the next day but apart from that that there wasn't much to do. Any luggage that was going to the station had to be packed long before. The leaving boys had sold the contents of their rooms days ago and had also done their major packing. In any House you walked into you would see and smell much the same scene, a long passage abounding in thrown-out paper and old notebooks, an occasional belated trunk or play-box heavily roped, a good deal of dust and one or two rather bored boys sitting round the gramophone.

Most people went down to Aunt Meredith's some time during the last afternoon not so much to buy something to eat, for by this time there was very little left, but because in the neighbourhood of Aunt Meredith's you were certain to bump into people from other Houses, and you could make final arrangements for meeting them in the holidays. Yes, one could pass quite a bit of time there lying on the grass in an ever-growing and diminishing group, pretending to watch the scratch cricket game taking place. Most of the boys lying there, watching the game in an absent-minded way, had little idea which side was batting and no idea of the score. It was one of those irritating things about lying in front of Aunt Meredith's that you could never quite see the scoreboard.

Slightly away to one side lying in the sun was Richard. He was not so much the centre of the group as just a part of it. John and Michael were lying there on the grass and so was Hugh. Lying just beyond Richard were Roger and both the Pauls from Campbell's House. Michael was wearing his absurd blue and white scarf as always in spite of the fact that the sun was mostly out, and Robert was feebly tugging one end of it. Robert was looking very young, much younger than his fifteen years. John was sitting cross-legged, and happy. It was an unofficial and unpremeditated tea-party consisting of coffee and spam sandwiches.

"Oh look. There's Harry."

Harry arrived balancing his cup in one hand and a plate of sandwiches in the other and trying to eat a sandwich at the same time; he eventually managed to settle himself down without disaster, next to John.

"Anyway, Harry, what on earth were you looking so grim about over there? Has Alex been rude to you or something?"

"Well, as a matter of fact, I was thinking that I was really very depressed and sad at leaving Chelborough. I've always mostly looked forward to going, but now that the time has come, it doesn't feel so good. It seems absurd to think that, although one always remains officially a Chelburian, one ceases to be anything except a welcome or unwelcome stranger as soon as one ceases to be here. Look, Richard, after about the first week or two of next term you won't really miss Michael or Harry or me. You'll be awfully glad to see us, of course, but most of your thoughts will be with Alex and Reggie and Roger, Rowland and Ronald and the small fry like the two absurd Pauls and Robert here. It's true, isn't it?"

"You'll make a great mistake, John, if you go traipsing through life imagining that everyone's reactions will be the same as yours. I should say that for the first month or two of next term you will be thinking of us rather more than we shall be thinking of you, and after that it will be about equal with the balance perhaps rather in our favour."

Michael looked up at John. "Well, I agree with you, John. I feel just the same. Here, Richard, what are the hymns in chapel tonight? Not that awful 'those returning make more faithful than before.'– not that, for heaven's sake."

"Lord of all faithfulness, Lord of all light "

"Richard, aren't we going to have that Irish hymn. You know – 'He leadeth me, He leadeth me, the quiet waters by' with the trebles going all sad at the same time?"

"Yes, we're having that too."

"It's too much," said Michael. "I shall weep. I nearly weep on ordinary nights with that hymn, but tonight: as a sad leaving boy, I shall weep buckets and buckets."

"I'm going to preach."

"Going to preach! Richard, don't preach. Please don't preach." Roger looked appealingly at Richard. "It'll waste such a lot of time. After chapel on the last night is the best time of all and there's a mass to do."

"Oh, I feel like preaching. It won't be awfully long." I should think about seven minutes."

"Richard, don't pay any attention to Roger. Preach away. I'd like you to preach. "Harry was speaking. "Does anyone know you're going to preach? I mean, it's a bit unusual on the last night of the term. Are you going to make it a kind of established practice?"

"Well, I know I'm going to preach and you know I'm going to preach. I don't know if anyone else knows."

Just at that moment there was a burst of applause from the long wooden annexe on the far side of Aunt Meredith's.

"What on earth's going on there? Is it a fag's-tea or something?"

"No, that's old Rattlebones standing his eleven cricketing heroes tea, in honour of their glorious victory in the Cock match. I expect he's just made a speech or something."

Roy Hodgson, the Head of the School, suddenly seemed to appear from nowhere.

"Hello, Richard, Can I say goodbye to you? I shan't be able to get up to see you tonight after Chapel."

"Yes, rather. Still, do come up any time, if you have a moment. I shall be up till very late." It was a tradition at Chelborough for the leaving boys to wander round till all hours on the last night saying goodbye to the masters.

"Well, I'll try, but I can't promise. I shall be some time with the Headmaster."

"You're going into the Guards, aren't you? Look, go and get yourself a cup of coffee and join us."

"No, I won't if you don't mind. I'm terribly busy. Well, goodbye Richard, in case I don't see you. And thanks a lot."

"Good luck to you."

Roy Hodgson sauntered off.

"Pompous ass," said Harry. "I hate Roy."

"Oh, I don't know," Richard said. "I rather like him."

And the chatter went on and the cricket match went on and the hours went by very, very slowly, except for the leaving boys, and for them the clock seemed to hurry indecently. It wasn't that they had anything in particular to do.

Peter Campbell had told Dickie and Reggie about his decision. He'd also told Dickie to put up a notice saying that he wanted to see everyone in the House at nine-thirty. There was nothing strange in that, but the instruction was a little unusual. "Will anyone who wishes to see me about anything, trivial or important, please come through before 9.30 pm as I shall not be available afterwards except in cases of extreme urgency."

Butler had agreed that Campbell should tell his House late on the last night that he was going. It was a little awkward, as his successor had not yet been decided upon. Dickie had been undisguisedly upset when Campbell told him the news, and Reggie had rather gulped his promise of temporary secrecy.

Campbell had vaguely thought out what he should say but he hadn't got it all clearly in his head. He was hoping he wouldn't make a fool of himself. Chapel had taken rather longer than usual and it was very soon after Chapel that Dickie came through to Campbell.

"They're all there, Campbell. Are you ready?"

"Just a moment, Dickie. I had a bit of paper with things written down on it. God, where is it? Oh, it doesn't really matter. Perhaps it will be easier without a bit of paper. Go ahead Dickie. Lead the way."

Yes, they were all there, drawn up as though for House prayers. Campbell was glad that they stood one behind each other in single file, so that you couldn't really see them all. He gave a rather feeble smile as he walked by. He stood in the middle of the passage under the bright light. It made him look much balder than he really was. The boys were obviously in fairly high spirits. One or two were leaning with their backs against the wall. He could see Roger, three away and looking very blasé.

"I've got rather more than usual to say tonight, so you may as well settle down and stop shuffling."

This was unusual. The shuffling stopped and the boys were very quiet. Roger stood up away from the wall.

"Well, first, I want to say that I think we've only had a fairly good term. I'm not judging by material successes but by your general attitude. We've had too many successes in recent terms, and the result is that many of the younger ones are beginning to take things too much for granted; some of you, who should be doing so, are not playing enough part in the life of the School. In House you're all right, but you're content with that. It's no good belonging to a good House and making it a good House, unless you're prepared to spread it all around a little more widely. I've told you this before and I'm going to tell you again that happiness isn't a well out of which you just draw things. You can't achieve it that way. It's an unsolicited return you get only in the measure in which you are prepared to do things, because they are worth doing. One or two of you I have noticed getting bored too easily and far too quickly. You seem to demand happiness as a kind of right. You keep on looking for it and then get angry because it isn't there."

Alex blew his nose very noisily and vigorously. There was a slight shuffle of feet, but Campbell didn't seem to notice.

"Reggie, as you know, is going to be Head of House next term, and I told him last week, and I tell you all now, that you've all got lots to do, if you want to keep this a really happy House and a successful. House, in the real sense of the word. You're probably tired of hearing me tell you that a House doesn't consist of the dormitories, the changing rooms and the studios. It doesn't consist of the cups that are won or lost; it just consists of people. You're it. Every term there are changes; some leave and some new boys come, but those of you who are here at any given moment are the House. A House cannot live on tradition or success, it lives only in the lives that you live here."

Campbell took out his handkerchief and wiped his forehead. He also wiped the corner of his right eye.

"I'm not going to say goodbye to Dickie and David in public; there's no need for us to wish them luck. They know what we all feel, and so I'll come to the harder part and you'll have to forgive me if I don't manage to express myself very well."

The shuffling stopped and there was complete silence. Campbell had been looking down at his feet. He looked up. He could see Charlie and

Paul Stocker. He vaguely saw Reggie standing at the far end, and he felt Dickie standing opposite him. Campbell looked down again.

"I want to tell you that I'm leaving Chelborough. I'm leaving now."

Nobody moved.

"I'm going at my own wish. I feel that I can do no more for you here, and it's better to let someone else have a try. I don't know yet for certain who will succeed me, but I have a shrewd idea that it's going to be someone who is both a good man and a nice man and a young man. I'm not going to pretend that I'm not sorry to be leaving you. That would be silly. You know I am, but I console myself that in fact – 'There is no parting from friends, but only from the ways of friendship.'"

"I shan't come back to Chelborough so long as any of you are still here, but I hope you will find time to write to me. Not often, just occasionally write to me here. This address will always find me, and, of course, I'll answer your letters."

Campbell stopped. He didn't know what to say.

"Tell your parents, if you care to, when you get home and tell them, too, that I'll be writing to them almost at once. I've asked you not to come through tonight unless it's really vital, because I wanted to say goodbye to all of you together. If you do come through you'll find the little 'Do not disturb' notice on the door. If you really want me, give two little knocks and I'll unlock the door. You see, I shan't want to see anyone else for a bit after this."

There was another slight pause and Campbell waited a moment. It was still; pitch-quiet, rather uncanny.

"I hope you won't think me sentimental if I say that I'll always remember each one of you and, of course, I can't help hoping that you'll always remember me. You'll forgive me quoting the poets just this once. I don't really know quite what to say. Perhaps just this –

O never weep for me, my love,
Or seek me in this land:
But light a candle for my luck
And bear it in your hand.

Campbell looked up at nobody in particular and smiled.

"Well, hey-ho, children. Good luck. Goodnight." They were all very silent as he walked out. Not many of them were looking up.

And so Peter Campbell returned to his room and locked the door. He went to the cupboard and looked for some beer, but there wasn't any there. But I don't want the stuff anyway. He lit a cigarette. I'm glad Richard preached. He was damned good. I suppose I shall join up. No, I swore I wouldn't think about that till after tomorrow.

Campbell went inside and locked the door once more. He walked over to the bookcase and picked up his photo album. He carried it over to Cleopatra, sat down and began idly looking through it. Damn, I wish now that Harry hadn't taken away that photo of Bill.

Afterword

Wellington College, in its first century, represented the apogee of training in Victorian and Edwardian manliness. The door was firmly shut on male experience of emotions in late Victorian England, with the Imperial cult of the stiff upper lip in the ascendant. Gay sex was pathologised as homosexual, as degenerate and as effeminate. Since the seventeenth century, upper class fathers had been sending boys away from home to "make a man of them". For a very long time, parents in the forces or Imperial service had no choice but to board their children in Britain. Harry Spencer, who arrived at Wellington in 1940, tells a familiar story in his memoir *Lascombe*. Moving from the nursery to boarding school seemed to him "the most natural thing in the world." He understood the notion that it was "essential to produce cultivated, resourceful and self-sufficient young fellows, who could live by themselves in the bush or lead their men in and out of tight corners all over the world. It was not even desirable that too sentimental a relationship should exist between parents and children," Spencer writes. His mother's reservations were quickly overcome.

Edward White Benson (1859-1872) was followed as Master by Edward Wickham (1873-1893), Bertram Pollock (1993-1910) and William Vaughan (1910-1937), all whom left their mark on the College, often for worse rather than better, including the insufferable Pollock. In this period, Wellington became a closed society. Years of seclusion made the College's mores and cultures absolute. Benson had created, out of fear of their inner natures, a lasting tradition of control over every boy. Pollock reinforced this. Yet between 1918 and 1939, English public schools, wrote Rollo Talboys, who arrived to teach in 1894, "secluded within their walls and playing fields, entered upon a period of eminent prosperity, renewal and expansion". They seemed "strongholds of survival and orderly tradition". Wellington, in contrast, "moved to a rhythm of curious passivity".

Rollo Talboys called his chapter in his history of the school about F.B.Malim's Mastership from 1921 to 1937 'Groundswell', which shows he knew something was amiss. What Wellington then lacked, so obviously beneficial later, was a formally recognised second master, able to represent the Common Room to the Master and vice versa. One can reconstruct what Talboys's 'Groundswell' was. It in fact emanated in part from him, an intelligent observer of the school's Common Room characters. A predictable struggle for power, which had its origins in Pollock's urbane and superior view of his Mastership, marred Malim's long reign. The Common Room expanded with fifty-three new appointments. Graham Stainforth, a foundationer boy and then head of the Beresford, noted that "for many years after Pollock's sour relations with his staff there remained an uneasy atmosphere at times". When he returned in to teach in 1935, the 'Old Guard' of tutors then consisted of Tomlinson, Eustace, Larmour, all from Pollock's days, together with the monstrous Mr Wanstall, known universally as the Hun.

There were three people, one boy and two masters, Giles Romilly, Cuthbert Worsley and Robin Gordon Walker, who, in their different ways, challenged Malim's regime directly. Opposite them stood the 'Old Guard', five of them senior tutors. Worsley, twenty-two years old, arrived in 1929 and his first mistake was asking boys in his form to tea. He was read a "firm but polite lecture by the three tutors concerned on the moral dangers of such association, both mine with the boys and that of boys from different dormitories with each other." He quickly learnt that there was war on about who owned the boys in his form: "they're not your boys and don't you think it! It's the tutor's job to see to their development."

Giles Romilly, arriving in the Blucher in Lent 1931, was a highly intelligent boy. His tutor was C.M. Hughes-Games, one of Malim's first appointments in 1921, who had won an MC in the Great War. Romilly was told he should not make friends outside the Blucher: "I like boys to find friends in their own dormitory", Hughes-Games insisted. His inner rebellion began with the issue of "dormitory spirit", which he called "team spirit gingered up and applied in regions where it was quite unnecessary". He was indoctrinated to believe that "any friendship between an older and younger boy was immoral".

The issue of school caps, touching sacred tradition, mattered hugely to the 'Old Guard'. Their battle over this with Worsley became a signal defeat; they doubtless never forgave him. Ink-stained, filthy and much used as weapons, bullies pinched the caps; weaklings suffered for the beatable offence of being caught bareheaded. The 'Old Guard' was cloistered, fighting a losing battle in the Lodge in the evening when school caps were discussed. The decree went out: wearing of caps was abolished within school grounds. By 1933, Worsley's rooms had become the place for young intellectuals, like Giles Romilly, to drop in, talk and play his gramophone. His tutor tried to forbid Romilly from doing this. No wonder, when Romilly's book, *Out of Bounds*, taking the lid off life at Wellington blew up nationally, many in the Common Room assumed mistakenly that Worsley had been some kind of agent provocateur.

Intensive control of the boys' time was the doctrine that held the 'Old Guard' together. The brooding suspicion was that mutual boy sex was endemic, that, given the faintest chance in this monastic atmosphere, their carnal appetites would take over. The Hun looked "at every boy", joked Talboys, "as if he suspected he was going to have a baby." One highly respected master from 1937 to 1943, confessed to his memory of Wanstall in old age: "I am not ashamed even now to confess that I really was scared".

Summarising his first years in the Common Room 1935 to 1937, Gus Stainforth recorded that "two charismatic figures and several other stormy petrels, encouraged by Talboys, then dangerously shook the iron framework of the old disciplines". Robin Gordon Walker was in the Hardinge from 1924-8, then returned to teach history soon after Worsley's arrival. Michael Howard, OW, describes his charisma: "small, dark, bald, restlessly energetic, Robin dragged us along by his own enthusiasms: he flirted outrageously with the more attractive boys...his endless supply of chocolate biscuits were at our entire disposal... we listened in thrall as he read to us ... we were discovering love, and were at that Titania-like stage when we lavished our affections on the first object in sight, which, in the absence of girls, was one another... all this Robin looked on with benevolent approval". He wanted to enhance and celebrate the teenage emotional lives of boys, encouraging their interest in art and literature. Many recall his teaching and the remarkable inspiration of his personality.

Not for nothing did Malim call himself "an impenitent Victorian". His famous cri de coeur was "there is no such thing as sex at College and if there is I knock it hard on the head". He believed strongly in dormitories run by men with "the sympathy, insight and the personality" which "wins loyalty and confidence" in young boys, but Gus felt he was a man "running out of steam and patience." Malim's achievement, said Gus, was "to hold Wellington firm, industrious and disciplined, with husbanded resources", enabling numbers to grow: the school roll grew from 553 to 660 between 1921 and 1937.

Graham Stainforth wrote in his memoir "I viewed with no little dismay the arrival of Bobby Longden". His tense reaction to the new Master was explicable in view of his own Wellington career there. Seldom can one era in the life of a school have been so dramatically replaced by another, as when Malim was replaced by Longden in September 1937. However, Howard narrates, there came instead, in Malim's place, Apollo: "a beautiful young bachelor, slim and golden-haired, aged only thirty-three". It was Talboys, primarily, who saw Longden into Wellington, dropping his inveterate mask and showing himself as a reformer in doing so. 'Desiderium' was the significant title he chose for the final chapter of his history of the school. Talboys realised that here was a man who would bring "the pervading vitality of his own youth, his sensitive and roving mind and his swift approach" to the school's problems. Above all, he wrote, Longden "was a rebel against all accepted notions, and it was in his gift for instant and intuitive contact, with ordinary individuals and with the school collectively, that he excelled".

Harry Spencer wrote about how the new Master was "young, brilliant and much loved by the boys". But David Newsome noted in his 1959 history that, when the appointment was announced to the Common Room, "many were disturbed". There were people who said he was "very Etonian". They feared he might lack "the weight and depth of character which really counted in making a lasting impression on a school". Gus's final verdict was double edged. Longden was "a man of great elegance and charm, a bachelor for whom life had run rather too easily." He was candid that one "soon fell for his genius for friendship".

However, Gus later concluded decisively, that "a darling of the Gods, Bobby Longden was really too nice to be a headmaster; he opened too many windows too quickly, causing draughts". As early as 1939, Gus thought Longden was "heading for serious trouble". His startling private comment to a colleague with whom he was good friends was "you cannot flirt with a great school". Longden was supported fully by the two OW bachelors, Robin Gordon Walker and the chaplain Geoffrey How." Michael Howard gives us an attractive portrait of How, appointed by Longden in his second year. He had worked as Warden of the Tonbridge Mission in the East End of London: "a quiet Anglican priest who radiated a quality of gentle devotion which gradually penetrated the chapel services." For sensitive adolescents, Howard found, seeking a faith, he was irresistible. Yet the going was tough. Longden had no head for money. Moreover he was something of an aesthete, lavishing expenditure of his own on the Lodge. His parties for senior boys were legendary. In December 1938, Longden had to deal with an outbreak of infantile paralysis. He leant heavily that Christmas on two colleagues: the stalwart E. G. as Gould was known, with thirty years of service to the school, and the chaplain Geoffrey How.

Harry Spencer's account of 8th October 1940 is vivid. Night after night he had been woken by the eerie wailing of the sirens; the trudge down to the shelters became routine. This particular night, after about ten minutes, "we heard huge explosions and we had visions of our dormitories in heaps of rubble." There were whispers and rumours, before "the hideous news emerged: the Master had been killed. No one else had been hurt. There were craters all along South Front". Gus remembered the "overwhelming and almost hysterical sense of loss". Even the most realistic and unemotional of us missed his bright presence; a vase of flowers was daily placed in his empty stall in chapel." "He inspired the school with a zest for life which no one who was at Wellington at that time can forget," wrote David Newsome. The aftermath of Bobby Longden's brief reign is a crucial aspect of the Wellington story.

From October 1940 until July 1943 the struggle for Wellington's soul went underground. The 'Old Guard', bemused, marshalled its forces. A new Master was for them another chance to regain ground it felt had been lost, while Geoffrey How and Robin Gordon-Walker had courted Longden. This is a story that has never been properly told. It has taken me more than a year and the help of others to disentangle it. After "the cold and remote" Malim, Michael Howard explains, Longden was not just "universally acceptable" to the boys, but "especially to the sixth, with many of whom he established relations of deeply affectionate friendship. These friendships were entirely innocent, but they reinforced the atmosphere of homoeroticism that was becoming prevalent at the end of the 1930s: a golden Platonic haze that protected us from the intrusions of an increasingly menacing world."

Wilfrid House, brought from Trinity College, Oxford to rescue Wellington in April 1941 as its new Master was a mixture of don and soldier. He had earned a DSO and MC in the Great War and then taught at Oxford. "The contrast could not have been greater," said Stainforth, who became a strong ally to House, "and had no use", one colleague wrote later, "for Gordon Walker." He met regularly at break with sound 'senior men' like Sumner Scott, appointed in 1912, Tancock, appointed in 1918 and E.G. In effect Gus had joined the 'Old Guard' by rallying to House. He recalled, much later in 1983, how "I grew to like and respect House as a man. I take this opportunity to acknowledge a personal debt to him and the service which in his unspectacular way he rendered Wellington at one of the gravest crises in her history".

House undoubtedly saw Gus as a very dependable lieutenant. He chose him to move to the Hopetoun in April 1943, at a difficult moment, when he had sacked Wanstall and was faced in the Common Room, Gus recorded, with "increasing hostility and bitter disagreements involving senior boys". The case of Wanstall required from him, David Newsome noted, "both courage and total integrity". The fall of the Hun came at last, after it was revealed that he had for years been beating boys across his knees and molesting them at the same time. House was modest, diffident and conscientious. Not a forceful speaker or a commanding personality, he pondered the crisis he felt was overtaking his Mastership. He became worried about the feud that had developed between the 'Old Guard' on the one hand and How and Gordon Walker on the other.

One of Longden's last acts had been to make Robin Gordon Walker tutor of the Hardinge. He proved quite unconventional by any standards, putting friendship with his boys above discipline, reversing all that was most sacred in Wellington tradition. Geoffrey How believed all boys were part of his parish. He had his own system for keeping tutors at bay, when they queried his late night meetings with boys who he felt needed his care, support and advice. Several of the 'Old Guard' became more frequent visitors to the Master, revealing how they were becoming engaged in bitter struggles to maintain their control over particular boys. Now running the History sixth, Gordon Walker had a claim on supervision of a boy's academic future, How could always claim their spiritual needs were his province.

House was a wartime Master run off his feet. He had no time to get to know any boys except a few of his prefects. He saw disunity among his staff as bad for morale. The enmity of the 'Old Guard' towards the young radicals became his preoccupation. He could not run the school, as a newcomer himself, with half a dozen senior men in revolt. He had to side firmly with the 'Old Guard'. Near the end of the summer term in 1943 he nerved himself for decisive action. He thought he could contain rebellion by removing How and mollifying Gordon Walker. But he miscalculated. The chaplain, stunned, accepted his dismissal. But Robin stood by How, resigning himself with immediate effect. He told the Hardinge boys about his decision on the last night of term. At an August camp at Tetbury, for those for whom Wellington had suddenly turned sour, there were sad goodbyes. Some of the closest friends of Robin and Geoffrey, including Spencer were both at this camp and later attended a party in London to celebrate Geoffrey's induction to an Essex benefice.

The row House faced with recent OWs, friends of his two scapegoats, was enormous and prolonged. A challenge to House, penned by an OW who had been one of Longden's school prefects, circulated widely in September 1943. Counting Longden as a "personal friend", the author of the document felt "the tradition which he had established was in good hands", even if "his policy suffered all the disadvantages of the pioneer." Letters of protest poured in to Lord Derby, chairman of the Governors: he interviewed four of them over tea at Claridges. The postbag of the

Vice-Chairman. Lord Wigram, was equally full. At Wellington itself, Harry Spencer and Alan Gore, juniors but devoted admirers of their tutor, staged a futile adventure in loyalty to him. Creeping into the chapel, they placed copies of a protest sheet in the hymn books. When Robin summoned them they quickly confessed: "it was scary creeping about in the dark", explained Harry, "we had torches but there was just enough light from the windows and it didn't take long at all." Robin explained their action to the Master as a silly prank and it was forgotten.

It is seldom in this story that we are able to hear the voice of the ordinary Wellingtonian. The House Books, traditionally confidential records, are not shown to any members of Common Room, and are handed on from one senior Head of House to the next. Writing in the autumn of 1943, as he struggled to hold the Hardinge together, John White recorded the "terrible feeling of loss" at Robin's departure, "not only for ourselves but for the whole of college, the terrible ill-feeling for the Master among Wellingtonians past and present," his "personal intense anger with Harry House". John White grasped at straws: even in their distress the jallies had voted the Hardinge "the most efficient washers up"; their landwork efforts had been "very creditable"; the Hardinge CCF platoon was "one of the best". Robin, he declared, would have been proud of them.

Gus Stainforth became Master of Wellington in January 1956. While Gus was always appreciative of House's achievement, he believed that he would have to do more to strengthen the foundations of Wellington's record and repute. One of his first head boys imbibed from him the notion that this was a school which "needed picking up by its bootstraps after the rather murky period in its history after the war." The place had become "rather like an amiable jellyfish", an OW governor told him. "The world was not hungering for Wellingtonians", Gus reminded himself; "the old markets for them had gone". It became Gus's ambition to raise the intellectual standing of the school. Reporting to the Governors in 1958, he regretted "our Achilles heel, lack of academic distinction". In May 1962 the Governors formally asked the DES to make a "special inspection" of the school, with a focus on further academic development. He was pleased that the number of Oxbridge scholarships was increasing and was especially appreciated the inspectors' congratulation in 1962 on the "wisdom and pastoral sense of the tutors" and their tribute to the school's house system.

Gus had always believed in a federal model, with tutors holding complete disciplinary control over every boy in his charge. In a sense, the 'Old Guard's' conception was very much how he ruled the school from 1956 to 1966. He was deeply traditional in his values, as his confidential memorandum "To all Members of Staff" in his last year as Master reiterates in detail. It is headed 'Discipline and Work'. All staff had "authority to beat a boy for misbehaviour" and all disciplinary beatings should be reported to the tutor and to him. Tutors were the very heart of the scheme. "If a boy is being troublesome, idle or generally unsatisfactory, his tutor should be told at once." But just as this draconian scheme of discipline was reissued in 1966, some heads of dormitories were working together to dismantle use of the cane by prefects at Wellington. Reform in the 1960s, it should be noted, was led by senior boys holding office as prefects, not by tutors, nor by magisterial edict.

In a final address to his fellow headmasters in March 1966, Gus reminded them of the principles that inspired his career in boarding schools, why he believed this was simply the best training there could be for elite manhood. A boy qualified for leadership by a long discipline of subordination. Being beaten, fagging or perhaps even standing to attention to speak to a prefect, reiterated the importance of the experience of subordination. Reaching what Gus called "the top of the feudal system", he then learnt about the exercise of responsibility and leadership. Graham Stainforth retained a grimly repressive structure of disciplinary control with some difficulty, in the age of the Beatles, *Lady Chatterley's Lover*, which he banned, and Philip Larkin's invention of sexual intercourse. He might have argued it was in his nature to play safe. Gus really did think a Wellingtonian in 1970 would have been lost in the school of 1950. For, twenty years before, "public schools were tightly woven introspective communities, demanding a high degree of conformity, insisting on inflated standards of behaviour and harbouring a feudal system based on artificial steps: e.g. senior boys could have their jackets undone etc. Fagging, beating, compulsory games, carefully organised spells of misery, were all held to be legitimate pressures for character building." Academic standards were respected less emphatically than other qualities: the world wanted "a decent chap, a gentleman and preferably an athlete."

I have discussed Masters, the Common Room, prefects and boys. I have tried to demonstrate the complexity of the power relationships at Wellington. There is another story of course, of five more Masterships and of the reforms since 1966, which have created the new Wellington of 2015. The school is now a fully coeducational institution and we should rejoice that this transition has been completed. We should congratulate the retiring Master Sir Anthony Seldon on the skill with which he has led Wellington into a new age, fostering core values which, so importantly, have been chosen by the whole community, the values of courage, integrity, respect, kindness and responsibility.

ANTHONY FLETCHER,
June 2015